GENOCIDE

When Is Intervention Necessary?

Lila Perl and Erin L. McCoy

Cavendish Square

New York

Published in 2020 by Cavendish Square Publishing, LLC
243 5th Avenue, Suite 136, New York, NY 10016

Library of Congress Cataloging-in-Publication Data

Names: Perl, Lila, author. | McCoy, Erin L., author.
Title: Genocide : when is intervention necessary? / Lila Perl and Erin L. McCoy.
Description: First edition. | New York, NY : Cavendish Square Publishing,
2020. | Series: Today's debates | Includes bibliographical references and index.
Identifiers: LCCN 2018056900 (print) | LCCN 2018059080 (ebook) | ISBN
9781502644763 (ebook) | ISBN 9781502644756 (library bound) | ISBN 9781502644749 (pbk.)
Subjects: LCSH: Genocide--History--Juvenile literature. | Genocide--Prevention--Juvenile literature.
Classification: LCC HV6322.7 (ebook) | LCC HV6322.7 .P465 2020 (print) | DDC 364.15/1--dc23
LC record available at https://lccn.loc.gov/2018056900

Editorial Director: David McNamara
Copy Editor: Michele Suchomel-Casey
Associate Art Director: Alan Sliwinski
Designer: Christina Shults
Production Coordinator: Karol Szymczuk
Photo Research: J8 Media

The photographs in this book are used by permission and through the courtesy of:
Cover, Mas@qur Sohan/NurPhoto/Getty Images; p. 4 European Commission DG ECHO, Flickr (https://
www.flickr.com/photos/69583224@N05/8022575954)/File: Darfurians refugees in Eastern Chad.jpg/
Wikimedia Commons/CCA-SA 2.0. Generic; p. 10 Archive Photos/Getty Images; p. 14 DEA Picture Library/
De Agostini/Getty Images; p.17 Photo12/UIG/Getty Images; p. 21 MPI/Getty Images; p. 24 National
Geographic Image Collection/Bridgeman Images; p. 28 Everett Collection Historical/Alamy Stock Photo;
p. 34 National Photo Company Collection, Library of Congress/File: Henry Morgenthau LCCN2016827675.jpg/
Wikimedia Commons/Public Domain; p. 36 Hanay, own work/File: Armenian Genocide Museum-Institute 7.jpg/
Wikimedia Commons/CCA-SA 3.0 Unported; pp. 40, 43 Universal History Archive/UIG/Getty Images; pp. 47, 57
Bettmann/Getty Images; p. 52 D. Gray/AP Images; p. 59 Apic/Hulton Archive/Getty Images; p. 65 © Tim Page/Corbis/
Getty Images; p. 67 Extraordinary Chambers in the Courts of Cambodia (https://www.flickr.com/people/39971069@
N02)/Flikr, uploaded by FishInWater/File: Nuon Chea, December 5, 2011.jpg/Wikimedia Commons/CCA-SA 2.0
Generic; p. 68 ELBAZ/Sygma/Getty Images; p. 77 J. Sciulli/WireImage/Getty Images; p. 79 Scott Peterson/Liaison/
Getty Images; p. 83 David Turnley/Corbis/VCG/Getty Images; pp. 89, 93 Antoine Gyori/Sygma/Getty Images; p. 97
Fred Ernst/AP Images; p. 100 Majority World/UIG/Getty Images; p. 103 Allison Joyce/Getty Images; p. 110 Chaideer
Mahyuddin/AFP/Getty Images; p. 114 Piroschka van de Wouw/AFP/Getty Images; p. 119 Office of the U.S. Chief of
Counsel for the Prosecution of Axis Criminality/Still Picture Records LICON, Special Media Archives Services
Division (NWCS-S) NARA/File: Defendants in the dock at the Nuremberg Trials.jpg/Wikimedia Commons/Public Domain.

Printed in the United States of America

CONTENTS

INTRODUCTION

Those who have survived the ongoing genocide in Darfur, a region of the African country of Sudan, have horrific stories to tell. One recalls what the men who attacked her told her: "They were shouting and screaming at us. You know what they were saying? 'We have come here to kill you! To finish you all! You are black slaves! You are worse than dogs.' The worst was that they were laughing and yelping with joy as they did those terrible things."

Stories as horrible as this one—sometimes even worse—are not hard to come by in Darfur, which translates to "Land of the Fur." The Fur people, along with the Masalit and the Zaghawa, are the region's major inhabitants, totaling six to seven million people. As many as

Opposite: Pictured in 2011, a refugee from Darfur sorts and cleans millet in a camp located 39 miles (56 kilometers) from the Sudanese border.

four hundred thousand men, women, and children living mainly as subsistence farmers and herders in this harsh, semiarid region of Africa have been murdered since 2003. Millions have been displaced from their homes, with thousands—sometimes hundreds of thousands—of new displacements taking place almost every year.

Genocide is the act of systematically killing a large group of people because of their race, ethnicity, nationality, or religion. And this genocide has, in many ways, never ended. Yet few of the world's nations have intervened in a way that could truly stop the violence. The question of how and when other countries should step in when a genocide is underway is a long-standing source of controversy. No one can deny that genocide is the most heinous of crimes. Yet none can agree on the moral obligations of those who find themselves looking on with horror.

Racism and Genocide

As a result of the long-standing racial prejudice of the central government toward the Darfuri, their homeland experienced years of neglect and marginalization. The Arab elite in Sudan have generally looked down on the *zurug* ("darkness of skin color") of others in their country. Darfur's inhabitants were taxed but were denied basic services, such as roads, schools, health care, and the chance for economic development. The government also failed to respond to the region's recurring droughts and resulting famines, despite the nation's increased prosperity due to its oil wealth.

However, in 2003, the government of Sudan took things a step further. It started to target Darfuris—a segment of its own population—for extermination and assigned deputies to carry out the task. The assailants were warriors mounted on horses or camels. Armed with guns and brazenly twirling their weapons in the air, these riders are known as "devils on horseback." Their name, Janjaweed, is believed by some to be derived from the

Arabic *jinn*, meaning "spirit," and *jawad*, meaning "horse"—thus, "evil horsemen." Or, the name may simply mean "warrior."

At the height of the genocide, the Janjaweed, supported by Sudanese president Omar Hassan al-Bashir and his administration, were charged with attacking the small villages of Darfur. These villages were often home to only a few hundred people, who were mainly of African (rather than Arab) descent. The Arab militiamen most often made their attacks in the early-morning hours. In some cases, the horsemen were preceded by government transport planes or by combat helicopters, which dropped improvised bombs. The aircraft created panic and disarray, making it easier for the Janjaweed to accomplish their goals of causing destruction and death on the ground. They burned villagers' houses, looted their belongings, stole their cattle, mutilated and murdered the men, sexually assaulted the women and girls, and left helpless babies to die. Homeless, the surviving villagers would end up in internally displaced persons (IDP) camps or wander across the border to refugee camps in the neighboring country of Chad.

Deliberate Slaughter

How does the mass murder of innocent civilians begin? In the 1930s and 1940s, in Nazi Germany, it sometimes began with a sharp rap at the door. This alarming sound was followed by the appearance of booted and uniformed officers armed with pistols. "We are the Gestapo. Come with us." That was the way many of the surviving Jews of this murderous campaign would remember the earliest government-sanctioned attacks against them.

At first, Nazi security squads made individual arrests. Jewish men who were law-abiding citizens were taken from their homes and families and sent to prisons and work camps. This was soon followed by mass arrests that included women and children, the very old, and the sick.

The Germans were both deliberate and systematic in slaughtering millions of people because of their ethnic heritage and their religion. They set up concentration camps where prisoners were often forced to perform slave labor and put to death in chambers filled with deadly gas. Their bodies would then be burned in ovens.

As a result, in a little more than six years—between 1938 and 1945—the Nazis murdered six million Jews from all over Europe in a genocidal campaign that later came to be known as the Holocaust. Five million other civilians whom the Nazis considered inferior to Germans were also put to death, among them Romany people (commonly known as Gypsies), communists, homosexuals, and people with disabilities. The word "holocaust," which comes from the Greek, means "wholly burnt" or "destroyed by fire."

Defining Genocide

A Polish Jew named Raphael Lemkin, who escaped the Nazi killing machine, later sought a word for the crime against humanity that had been committed. In 1943, Lemkin introduced it to the world's lexicon. Thenceforth all dictionaries would include the term "genocide." It is derived from *genos* (Greek for "race"; "kind") and *-cide* (from the Latin *caedere*, "to kill").

Genocide differs from civil and political wars, in which great numbers of both combatants and civilians die. Genocide has a particular aim: the deliberate murder of a racial, tribal, ethnic, national, or religious group, generally within a sovereign nation but also outside its borders, as in Nazi-occupied Europe.

Such mass murders have been going on since the earliest recorded history. The Old Testament, a part of both the Hebrew and Christian Bibles, recounts that God commanded the Israelites to "blot out" the tribe of the Amalekites from their land. Recorded history tells us of numerous religious genocides, such as the anti-Muslim and anti-Jewish Crusades and the Spanish Inquisition of the Middle Ages. Europeans' arrival in the Americas led to new instances of ethnic and racial genocide directed at Native Americans and at the population of African slaves on American soil. The twentieth century, despite its periodic claims to the attainment of global peace and human enlightenment, produced horrifying genocidal struggles and the greatest number of resulting deaths in history.

Should the International Community Intervene?

In the midst of ongoing violations of human rights by means of massacre, mutilation, maiming, sexual assault, and starvation, global citizens are left with the question of how they should react. To what degree are we morally obligated to inject ourselves into the situation? Why have most genocidal powers been allowed to fulfill their deadly goals, while others have been halted by outside forces?

In the case of Darfur, justice has yet to be achieved. Many Darfuris are still living in refugee camps more than a decade after being forced from their homes. In 2018, 1.76 million Darfuris— nearly one-third of Darfur's population—were still displaced, with new displacements happening almost every year. The International Criminal Court, an intergovernmental organization tasked with prosecuting international crimes against humanity such as genocide, issued a warrant for al-Bashir's arrest in 2009. The warrant accused al-Bashir of attacking his own people on a broad scale, making him the first sitting head of state to face such charges. Yet this international body had little power and no police force charged with carrying out such an arrest. As of 2018, al-Bashir remained president of Sudan.

Understanding the role that the rest of the world must play when a genocide is underway—and what nations even have the power to do—is a complicated task. It requires a broader knowledge of how genocides have been carried out over the course of history—and what people and nations have tried to do to stop them.

Chapter One

GENOCIDE IN THE AMERICAS

When Europeans arrived in the Americas beginning with the first voyage of Christopher Columbus in 1492, they discovered heavily populated lands. Many of the native peoples they encountered brought food to welcome the weary Spanish travelers. These men, as they explored the unfamiliar continents, would marvel at the sophistication of such complex and ancient societies as that of the Aztecs, whose metropolis of Tenochtitlán was described by Spanish explorers as the most beautiful city on earth.

However, when the Europeans arrived, death came with them. Over the next centuries, millions of Native Americans would die after being exposed to the diseases the Europeans carried. Disease was

Opposite: Samoset (*center right*), a member of the Abenaki nation, was reportedly the first Native American to encounter the pilgrims of the Plymouth settlement.

not the only killer, though. The Spaniards—and after them, the English and the Portuguese—would soon undertake a widespread campaign of murder and subjugation. They would steal the natives' lands and force them to work as slaves. They would kill them for small slights or even for entertainment. The Europeans considered themselves to be racially superior to Native Americans and believed that God supported their mission to dominate the Americas by whatever means necessary. This was, according to historian David E. Stannard, the "worst human holocaust the world had ever witnessed, roaring across two continents non-stop for four centuries and consuming the lives of countless tens of millions of people."

The many stories of this genocide appearing in this chapter offer devastating insight into what happens when nobody or almost nobody steps in to help. They can help us understand why so many people argue that, when a genocide is taking place, the world has an obligation to stop it. The question of who should stop it and how, though, remains more difficult to answer.

Colonialism and Genocide

The systematic and intentional murder of large groups of people because of their political, racial, or cultural associations has taken place since the days of the earliest humans. But it was not always called genocide. In fact, the term was not coined until after some of the most horrendous genocides of the twentieth century.

The unfortunate result of this is that many acts of mass murder that occurred before the twentieth century have not been referred to as genocides. As a result, we as students of history sometimes don't realize just how terrible these tragedies were. This is certainly true when it comes to the period of European colonialism in the Americas after the arrival of Columbus.

Colonialism is the act of taking control over another country or territory, sending settlers to occupy that area, and exploiting the resources that it has to offer, enriching oneself or one's nation in the process. Colonialism has taken place all over the world and has often involved violent acts on the part of the colonizers. With the European colonization of different territories of Africa came the brutal exploitation and enslavement of its peoples and the theft of its most valuable resources. But does colonialism necessarily involve genocidal acts?

Raphael Lemkin, who coined the term "genocide," describes it in such a way that sounds very much like colonialism: "Genocide has two phases: one, destruction of the national pattern of the oppressed group; the other, the imposition of the national pattern of the oppressor." In fact, according to genocide studies scholar A. Dirk Moses, "Lemkin hints that genocide is *intrinsically colonial* and that therefore settler colonialism is *intrinsically genocidal.*"

"Any colony tends to become one vast farmyard, one vast concentration camp where the only law is that of the knife," psychiatrist and philosopher Frantz Fanon writes. Fanon believed that colonialism was an inherently violent act and could only be overcome through the violent resistance of the colonized.

Others argue, though, that colonialist policies do not necessarily constitute genocide. Historian Jeffrey Ostler explains: "Conservative definitions emphasize intentional actions and policies of governments that result in very large population losses, usually from direct killing." The emphasis here is on targeted and intentional slaughter organized by a government.

Widespread societal beliefs in the superiority of Europeans drove the persecution and murder of countless Native Americans. Though a central or government authority did not always fuel this violence, Native Americans were targeted specifically because of their racial, ethnic, religious, and cultural backgrounds, just as the Jews were in World War II.

The Many Cultures of the Americas

It is difficult to know how many people lived in the Americas in the pre-Columbian (pre-colonization) era. Estimates range from as little as ten million to as many as one hundred million. What is known, though, is that they belonged to a complex web of groups and cultures spanning from the farthest reaches of the north all the way to Tierra del Fuego at the southernmost tip of South America. North America alone had an estimated eight hundred separate nations.

This rendering depicts what the Aztec city of Tenochtitlán may have looked like in the fifteenth century, before the arrival of Europeans.

Some lived in relatively small groups while others were part of vast networks of trade and confederation. The Mayan Empire comprised more than 100,000 square miles (258,999 square kilometers), was made up of at least fifty independent states, and lasted for more than one thousand years.

The city of Tenochtitlán, a crown jewel of the Aztec Empire, was located on an island the size of Manhattan in the center of a saltwater lake where modern-day Mexico City is located today. Long causeways connected the city to the mainland, and drawbridges connected houses over a web of canals. Canoes crisscrossed the lake, bringing merchandise to a great market where honey, fruits, deerskins, pottery, pies, eggs, feathers, timber, tiles, gold, silver, brass, and copper were sold. The city was lush with aviaries of exotic birds, dazzling gardens, and art. At the end of the fifteenth century, 350,000 people lived there, five times as many as in Seville or London.

The Inca Empire along the west coast of South America comprised almost a hundred different communities. Its city of Cuzco was clean and carefully engineered, home to between 150,000 and 200,000 people. Inca palaces were built of precious metal, wood, and marble and were equipped with enormous halls that could contain up to four thousand people.

Countless other civilizations, large and small, dotted the Americas and had histories dating back thousands of years.

It is important to dwell on this history to understand just how much was lost. Stannard, the author of *American Holocaust: The Conquest of the New World*, notes that in the colonial era (and even to this day) colonists chose to believe that there was little or no civilization there before them so that it seemed it was their intellectual and moral "right" to conquer the New World.

The Arrival of Columbus

On October 12, 1492, Columbus and his three ships first made landing on an island he called San Salvador in the modern-day Bahamas. There and on the other islands they visited during this first journey—modern-day Cuba and Hispaniola, home to Haiti and the Dominican Republic—Columbus encountered mostly friendly local nations. Yet he set about immediately searching for gold and kidnapped local men, women, and children to take back and put on display in Barcelona and Seville. Few survived the journey to Europe.

Columbus's second journey was in 1494, when he made landfall in Hispaniola with seventeen ships and 1,200 sailors, soldiers, priests, and colonists. Upon arrival, many immediately fell ill. The natives who came to welcome them with fruit and fish caught this illness, and it began to spread across the island. Soon, recalled writer and historian González Fernández de Oviedo, "all through the land the Indians lay dead everywhere. The stench was very great and pestiferous."

The Spaniards spread this disease further as they visited modern-day Jamaica and Cuba in their search for gold. It was then that the violence began. They committed widespread theft, rape, torture, and murder, killing more than fifty thousand Native Americans in the process. These assaults were often senselessly brutal. The Spaniards would tear babies away from their mothers and smash them against rocks or feed them to their dogs. In a village called Zucayo, where they had previously been welcomed with a feast, they began to kill people just to test the sharpness of their swords, starting a massacre that left twenty thousand Native Americans dead.

Many fled to other islands, including the Taíno chief Hatuey, who led a group of survivors to nearby Cuba. There, he told his people that the Spaniards worshipped gold and then threw the gold he had into a nearby river in the hopes of protecting them.

Christopher Columbus returns from his voyage to the Americas with Native Americans he has captured and forced to return with him.

The group was nonetheless found and either killed or enslaved. Hatuey was condemned to be burned alive. As he was being tied to the stake, a friar tried to convert him to Christianity so that his soul could go to heaven. Hatuey replied that if Spaniards went to heaven, he would rather go to hell.

In March 1495, Columbus organized raids that would kill thousands more. Dominican friar Bartolomé de las Casas, one of the few Spaniards to openly condemn such practices, recalls these massacres: "It was a general rule among Spaniards to be cruel; not just cruel, but extraordinarily cruel so that harsh and bitter treatment would prevent Indians from daring to think of themselves as human beings or having a minute to think at all."

Later, Columbus would divide the people and communities of the region under the rule of Spanish masters to work as slaves. They would be whipped and starved to death until, within just a few decades, their population was so reduced that the Spanish were forced to kidnap Native Americans from other islands and as far north as South Carolina to work as slaves in the Caribbean.

When Columbus arrived in 1492, an estimated eight million people lived on Hispaniola. Just four years later, the population had been reduced to four or five million. And by 1535, just forty-three years after the arrival of Columbus, the native population of Hispaniola was essentially extinct, with a few thousand left at most.

By the end of the sixteenth century, about two hundred thousand Spaniards had moved to the New World. Between sixty and eighty million Native Americans were dead.

Mexico and Central America

Nearly as soon as Hernán Cortés and his men encountered the stunning city of Tenochtitlán, they sought to conquer and subjugate its people. In 1519, with the support of an estimated 150,000 Tlaxcaltecs—nearby political rivals of Tenochtitlán—and less than one thousand Spaniards, Cortés entered the city under auspices of peace. However, once inside the city, they attacked, starting by killing the dancers and singers in a public celebration. After two weeks of struggle, Cortés and his men fled the city but left behind smallpox, which decimated most of the population within a matter of months. Then Cortés returned to seize the city.

Cortés was far from the only Spaniard to wreak havoc in Mexico and Central America. According to de las Casas,

Widespread Disease

By some estimates, exposure to new diseases such as smallpox, measles, and influenza (flu) killed an estimated 90 percent of the Native American population. This occurred over hundreds of years, as new areas were exposed for the first time with the arrival of European settlers. The Europeans were accustomed to epidemics; the black plague alone had killed as much as 60 percent of Europe's population in recent centuries. Indigenous populations, however, had never before been exposed to these diseases. For this reason, they hadn't developed immunity or resistance to them and were more likely to die of them.

Over time, native communities also developed immunity, but not before their populations had been dramatically reduced. Such was the case for Kalapuya and Chinook nations in the Pacific Northwest after an 1830s malaria epidemic. Their populations, according to Ostler, "were never allowed to recover. The reason was the advent of a new phase in the region's colonization: the coming of American missionaries and settlers with an intention to remake Indian country in their own image." They sought to convert Native Americans to Christianity and stole tribal lands. The 1850s gold rush in southwestern Oregon saw what Ostler calls "a war of extermination against Indians, a clear-cut case of genocidal intent."

So it was, then, that a combination of disease and violence left Native American populations decimated across two continents. It is nearly impossible to talk about one in isolation from the other.

the conquistador Pedro de Alvarado, along with his brothers and soldiers, "killed more than four or five million people in fifteen or sixteen years, from the year 1525 until 1540, and they continue to kill and destroy those who are still left; and so they will kill the remainder."

The Spaniards by now had trained their dogs to hunt Native Americans like animals, and this was sometimes done for entertainment. Sexual assaults and murder were widespread. Many Native Americans stopped having children or would even kill their babies to spare them from the pain of living as slaves. Seventy-five years after the Spaniards' first arrival, the population of central Mexico had fallen by 95 percent.

South America

Similarly, the arrival of the Spaniards in modern-day Peru and Chile would result in the death of 94 percent of the native population. There, the Spaniards continued their search for gold and riches. They would slowly bury people alive as they sought to extract the whereabouts of treasure they believed the Native Americans had hidden.

Enslavement of the local population in silver mines and on plantations soon became the norm. These slaves were worked to death simply because it was cheaper to replace them with other natives than to feed them. Most only survived three to four months at this labor. Such practices only slowed down around the mid-sixteenth century because the Spanish crown was fearful that its labor force would be too severely depleted.

North America

In 1607, 104 settlers established the first permanent English settlement in the Americas at Jamestown, Virginia. The settlers

Native Americans are depicted trading with settlers in Jamestown, Virginia, in 1609.

were impressed by the Native Americans' ability to produce huge amounts of food despite the sickness that was spreading among them. They had democratic councils and dignified leaders, and they were admired for their "peacefulness, generosity, trustworthiness, and egalitarianism."

British colonial leaders, however, saw Native Americans as people destined to be conquered. Captain John Smith, who helped establish Jamestown, called them "all Savage," adding that "Their chiefe God they worship is the Divell [Devil]." The Christian English believed that they had a God-given right to claim the land for themselves.

Organized violence toward the native population began within just a few years. Leaders such as Smith and Ralph Lane would kidnap Native American children and hold them hostage. They would burn down whole communities when they felt they had been slighted.

In 1610, Thomas West, 12th Baron De La Warr, governor of the Colony of Virginia, and his second-in-command, George

Percy, launched a brutal attack on Chief Powhatan and his people because they were accused of harboring English runaways. Percy ordered many to be beheaded, including women and children. He burned their houses down and had the corn in their fields destroyed.

After this attack, relations between the English and Native Americans were increasingly violent. Native Americans would approach the English with offerings of food, only to be imprisoned and executed. The English signed peace treaties with the intent of taking the Native Americans all the more by surprise the next time they attacked. Native Americans were killed in skirmishes, by mass poisoning, and by dogs trained to hunt them. Their fields were burned and their villages destroyed. The colonists desired to root them "out from being longer a people uppon the face of the earth." They were targeted because they were not white, not European, and not Christian.

By 1607, the population of Powhatan's people had already been reduced by at least 75 percent by the disease that previous European arrivals in the area had brought with them. By the end of the seventeenth century, another 95 percent of Powhatan's people had died.

Violence Escalates

The Pequot War, which began in July 1636 over the murder of a white settler, peaked with the English burning down a Pequot village as the people there slept. The English attackers recalled horrifying scenes of "women, children, and feeble old men" fleeing or crawling under their beds to escape the flames. As many as seven hundred died. Puritan minister Cotton Mather later recounted the event in words that reflected the way the settlers dehumanized the Native Americans: "these barbarians were dismissed from a world that was burdened with them."

Thousands more from the Narragansett and Wampanoag nations were killed in King Philip's War (1675–1676). Mather referred to one attack, in which hundreds were burned alive, as a "barbeque." Hunting Native Americans soon became akin to a sport in New England. Killing native women and children was common practice, one that Stannard argues was "flatly and intentionally genocidal. For no population can survive if its women and children are destroyed."

The United States' Founding Fathers also participated in this carnage. George Washington ordered the merciless destruction of Iroquois and Seneca settlements, earning the name "Town Destroyer" among those who survived. He, like many of his contemporaries, believed that Native Americans were little different than wolves, "both being beasts of prey, tho' they differ in shape." Thomas Jefferson ordered that any Native American group that stood in the way of US expansion be exterminated.

According to Stannard, while both the Spaniards and the English committed widespread genocide, their methods were different because their goals were different. The Spaniards wanted gold and riches, so all in all, it was not in their financial best interest to exterminate entire communities; rather, they would enslave them and force them to work in mines and on plantations, where they would die of overwork and starvation. The English, though, wanted land, so "in British America extermination was the primary goal, and it was so precisely because it made economic sense."

The Trail of Tears

Andrew Jackson, elected president in 1828, was famous for his brutality. He believed that "the whole Cherokee Nation ought to be scurged," or wiped out. During his presidency, Cherokee lands were seized by the state of Georgia. When the US Supreme Court

During the Trail of Tears, Native Americans were forced to relocate, as depicted in this 1993 lithograph by Herbert Tauss.

upheld the right of the Cherokee and other Indian nations to their lands, Jackson said of the Supreme Court justice who wrote the ruling, "John Marshall has made his decision, now let him enforce it." So the drive to steal native land continued without cease.

The passage of the Indian Removal Act in 1830 instigated what became known as the Trail of Tears. In 1838 and 1839, under the direction of General Winfield Scott, seventeen thousand Cherokee were forced into detainment camps, then driven in large groups by foot and by wagon westward. Government-sponsored enforcers of the march intentionally passed through areas where there were breakouts of cholera and other epidemics and fed the Cherokee spoiled food. More than eight thousand Cherokee died.

Members of the Cherokee, Seminole, Choctaw, Muscogee (Creek), Chickasaw, Ponca, and Ho-Chunk/Winnebago nations were all forced to relocate between 1830 and 1850.

A man who would later fight in the American Civil War recalled participating in this march: "I fought through the civil war and have seen men shot to pieces and slaughtered by thousands, but the Cherokee removal was the cruelest work I ever knew."

Westward Expansion

The Spanish arrived in modern-day California in the sixteenth century, bringing disease and violence with them. Religious missions established in the territory captured Native Americans and forced them to live in mission compounds in unclean and inhuman conditions. The missionaries there tried to convert them to Christianity. All the while, the Native American captives were forced to work on mission plantations, where they died in great numbers from malnutrition, overwork, and disease. They were whipped if they tried to escape.

California, along with large swaths of the American West, was ceded by Mexico to the United States in 1848. Shortly after, in response to a few thefts of livestock from white settlers, two successive California governors declared the need for a war of extermination against Native Americans. Between 1852 and 1860, 60 percent of indigenous Californians died at the hands of state-mandated genocidal policy.

Meanwhile, campaigns throughout the West backed by official US policies systematically stole Native American land and killed or displaced native nations. The Dawes General Allotment Act of 1887 called for splitting up reservation land between individual tribesmen to encourage them to live more like white farmers. Any land left over was offered up for public sale. The law weakened traditional tribal structures and tried to force many formerly nomadic tribes to live as farmers. It was another way to undermine Native American culture and propagate European ways of life.

Many Native American nations fought back against the constant westward expansion of the United States. However, by

1890, the Plains Indians were left mostly desperate and defeated, and in December of that year, a group of them chose to perform a Ghost Dance at Wounded Knee Creek in South Dakota, in the hopes that the religious ceremony would bring back the world that existed before the arrival of the Europeans. US authorities who were looking on interpreted it as a war dance. They arrested and killed the Lakota Sioux chief Sitting Bull, and the tribe fled. Thirteen days later, the Lakota were found and escorted back to Wounded Knee. As Colonel James Forsyth's cavalry tried to disarm them, they started the Ghost Dance again, and there was a scuffle when one young Lakota would not give up his rifle. US soldiers started to fire on the Lakota, leaving between 150 and 300 dead, including more than 60 women and children.

The Native Americans who survived this brutal, centuries-long campaign of westward expansion and land seizure were forced to live on reservations with limited rights to self-governance. They weren't granted US citizenship until 1924.

Native Americans Today

Today, there are 560 federally recognized tribes and more than 300 Native American reservations in the United States. These tend to have a higher density of poverty than the rest of the country. In fact, 26.2 percent of American Indians and Alaska Natives live in poverty, compared to just 8.8 percent of whites and 12.7 percent of all Americans, according to the 2016 US Census. Places such as the Pine Ridge Indian Reservation in South Dakota, occupied by the Oglala Sioux, have an 80 percent unemployment rate. There are no banks or libraries, and many homes lack basic resources such as electricity, water, and sewage systems.

Much of the poverty found on reservations stems from an economic system poorly equipped for tribal cultural values. For instance, because land on reservations is often held communally, individuals find it hard to establish credit, and without good credit it's hard to get a loan to start a business, build new infrastructure, or even buy a car. Meanwhile, federally funded schools attended by Native American children are often housed in dilapidated buildings, according to a 2014 article from Mic. At the Little Singer Community School in the Navajo Nation, students have to carry their chairs from class to class because it seems there aren't enough chairs to fill every classroom. Possibly as a result of this, student performance in these schools is far lower than the national average.

More than one in three Native Americans living in the United States today have personally experienced racism or racism-fueled violence directly or within their family, according to a 2017 poll. Three in four believe that Native Americans still face discrimination in the United States.

Native Americans throughout the Americas experience similar discrimination and have sometimes faced brutal assault by their own governments. Starting in 1980, the Guatemalan army carried out "Operation Sophia," a genocidal campaign targeting people of Mayan descent. Over the next three years, two hundred thousand people were either killed or made to disappear, and another 1.5 million were displaced from their homes as 626 villages were destroyed. A United Nations trust commission concluded in 1999 that, because the United States had helped train, arm, and finance the troops, it bore some responsibility for the genocide. The United States did not intervene to stop it.

Adolf Hitler, whose brutal Holocaust would kill six million Jews in the mid-twentieth century, "from time to time expressed admiration for the 'efficiency' of the American genocide campaign against the Indians, viewing it as a forerunner for his own plans and programs," Stannard writes. This centuries-long campaign of horror in the Americas would, instead of teaching the world a humbling lesson, go on to inspire more terror.

Chapter Two

THE ARMENIAN GENOCIDE

As the violence and brutality of World War I shocked and ravaged the world, yet another genocide was underway. It was remarkably similar to that of the Native Americans in the techniques that were used to systematically murder and subjugate the Armenians, a religious minority in modern-day Turkey. Armenians were subjected to forced labor, death marches, massacres, sexual assault, and starvation.

A Religious and Ethnic Minority

The Armenian genocide was committed between 1915 and 1918 by the Turkish rulers of what was

Opposite: A mother leans over her child, who has passed away. The child is one of many Armenians who died after being forced into the Syrian desert during the Armenian genocide.

then known as the Ottoman Empire, a sprawling Muslim state in the Near East. The victims of the genocide were the Armenians, a Christian people who had lived under the Ottoman Turks since the fourteenth century.

Armenians were permitted to administer their own school systems and to legislate matters of marriage and inheritance within their community. However, as *dhimmi*, or non-Muslims living under Muslim sovereignty, the Armenians had limited civil and religious rights. They were not allowed to practice their Christian religion and were forced to pay a special tax that was not levied on Muslims. In the Ottoman courts, they had almost no legal rights.

As it was not believed that Armenian men could be trusted to defend Islam in times of war, they were exempt from military service. Yet a longtime practice of the Ottomans had been the "collection" of boys from Christian families for the purpose of converting them to Islam. These youths could then be put to work serving in the Ottoman military and civil service. The taking of young boys from their families was known as *devshirme*.

Another demand of the Ottoman rulers was that Armenian families house Turkish army units, often for long periods through the winters. During their quartering the soldiers received the families' best lodging space and food and often abused their privileges by committing theft and sexual assault.

Rising Activism

Centuries of Armenian frustration and silence reached a breaking point in the mid- to late 1800s, as progressive ideas from the West seeped into the vast Ottoman domain. Contact with Europe and the United States through reading, study, and travel acquainted members of the repressed minority with the principles of human rights and liberty. American Protestant missionaries began to circulate through the Armenian communities of the Ottoman Empire.

The Armenian Apostolic Church, founded in 301 CE, had its own ceremonies and forms of worship, so its believers did not for the most part adopt the religious rituals of the American missionaries. However, the visitors from afar brought other benefits to the Armenian people. Many of the missionaries were female, and they advanced education for women, establishing schools, cultural centers, and colleges in key cities and provinces.

Liberal thought gave rise to Armenian activism. Secret societies as well as openly revolutionary political parties sprang up, aimed at wresting self-rule or at least a noncorrupt form of constitutional government from the Ottomans.

Sultan Abdülhamid II, who had ascended to the throne in 1876, was less than pleased with the increasing demands of the Armenians. The European powers had already condemned him for the massacres of his non-Muslim subjects in the Balkans, where Christian Serbs and Bulgarians were clamoring for independence. The people of the Balkan lands under Ottoman rule would eventually win their independence. The Armenians, though, were scattered throughout Ottoman Turkey. What was the answer to the so-called Armenian Question?

Precursors to Genocide

By the time the crumbling Ottoman Empire entered World War I in 1914 on the side of Germany, it had lost its numerous holdings in southeastern Europe, including Serbia, Bulgaria, and Greece. In an effort to reestablish the empire's former wealth and glory and to expand it in an easterly direction, a group of reforming patriots popularly known as the Young Turks forced the sultan to concede political power to them.

The Hamidian Massacres

Between 1894 and 1896, Sultan Abdülhamid II unleashed a series of savage attacks on the Armenian people in provinces all over the country and in Constantinople, the capital city today called Istanbul. For the purpose of terrorizing, looting, and murdering the Christian minority, the sultan created a force of more than sixteen thousand cavalry troops known as the Hamidiye regiments.

Scattered around the country in more than thirty regiments, the Hamidiye were drawn from the Kurdish population of the Ottoman Empire. Also a minority group, the Kurds were a nomadic, pastoral people who practiced their own form of Islam. In organizing the Kurdish horsemen to spread terror throughout the Armenian settlements, the sultan was using one minority group to subdue another. Kurds who did not comply were threatened with persecution. Those who cooperated said they had "received assurances that they will not be called to answer before the tribunals for any acts of oppression committed against Christians."

The Hamidian massacres erupted over Armenian protests against unreasonable and excessive taxation and over calls for equality with Muslims before the law. American missionary and relief workers reported sexual assaults on a massive scale; the bayoneting and shooting of men, women, and children; and houses set on fire.

In all, some two hundred thousand Armenians were murdered in the Hamidian massacres of 1894 to 1896. The United States, through the Red Cross and other humanitarian groups, sent aid to the survivors, who were dying of hunger and disease. European powers registered their protests through their foreign missions and their ambassadors. Yet the massacres played themselves out and would serve as a precursor for the Armenian genocide of 1915–1918.

The Young Turk political party was formally known as the Committee of Union and Progress (CUP). Its founders called themselves reformers, so the Armenian population of the Ottoman Empire hoped that their situation might improve under CUP rule.

The Armenians soon learned, however, that the Young Turk movement favored "ethnic cleansing"—ridding the nation of non-Turkish peoples. In the words of Mehmet Talaat, one of the triumvirate that then controlled the government, "Turkey belongs only to the Turks."

Genocide in the Military

Although Christian Armenian men were prohibited from serving in the military, it had been decided at the beginning of the war that they would be useful as labor battalions. Henry Morgenthau, the US ambassador to Turkey in 1915, described their duties and their treatment in his book, *Ambassador Morgenthau's Story*, published at the end of the war in 1918.

The Armenians "had been transformed into road labourers and pack animals. Army supplies of all kinds were loaded on their backs, and, stumbling under the burdens and driven by the whips and bayonets of the Turks, they were forced to drag their weary bodies into the mountains of the Caucasus."

In February 1915, however, following a humiliating defeat at the hands of the Russians, the Turkish government ordered the massacre of Armenian men in the army's labor battalions on the grounds that they had been supportive of the Russians. The slaughter of the former army laborers was vividly described by Morgenthau:

> *Here and there squads of 50 or 100 men would be taken, bound together in groups of four, and then marched out to a secluded spot a short distance from the village.*

Henry Morgenthau, US ambassador to Turkey in 1915, documented the atrocities of the Armenian genocide.

Suddenly the sound of rifle shots would fill the air, and the Turkish soldiers who had acted as the escort would sullenly return to camp. Those sent to bury the bodies would find them almost invariably stark naked, for, as usual, the Turks had stolen all their clothes. In cases that came to my attention, the murderers had added a refinement to their victims' sufferings by compelling them to dig their graves before being shot.

A Murderous Policy

By the spring of 1915, with the war in progress, the Turkish government launched its plans to slaughter the two to three million Armenian people who were living among the country's nearly thirty million Turks. The methods they used included roundups of able-bodied men who were either shot en masse by killing squads or marched away for deportation. The families they left behind—women and children, elderly and infirm relatives—were forced to leave their homes, taking only a few possessions.

Armenians would lose their lives in massacres; during death marches, in which they were forced to walk long distances without food or water until they collapsed; by being forcibly drowned in the Black Sea; or by being exiled in the harsh Syrian Desert. More Armenians are believed to have died in Syria—of thirst, starvation, and disease—than anywhere else.

April 8 saw the first deportation orders carried out. On April 24, the day before the Allied armies invaded Turkey, approximately 250 Armenian political leaders and intellectuals in Constantinople were rounded up and killed. Mass arrests in the capital followed. By May, more than 2,300 of the city's most distinguished Armenian residents had been apprehended and sent to the interior to be murdered by the state.

Although the British and French enemies of the Turks protested these and other crimes taking place throughout the country, they were busy waging war against the Turks' German allies. The United States was well informed about the atrocities taking place in Turkey. Morgenthau cabled the following message to the US State Department on July 16, 1915: "Deportation of and excesses against peaceful Armenians is increasing and from harrowing reports of eye witnesses it appears that a campaign of race extermination is in progress under a pretext of reprisal against rebellion."

By the end of 1915, close to one million Armenians were believed to have lost their lives to the genocide, which would continue until 1918 and claim a total of 1.5 million lives. Nor did Turkey's defeat and the conclusion of World War I mean the end of Armenian oppression. Massacres and expulsions were carried out between 1920 and 1922, leading to tens of thousands more victims of the fierce campaign.

Turkish Killing Squads

A new governmental body known as the Special Organization (SO) was tasked with carrying out the genocidal policies of the Ottoman state. The SO murdered Armenians en masse; destroyed homes, schools, and churches; appropriated Armenian property and other holdings; and blotted out all evidence of Armenian

Soldiers stand beside the bodies of Armenian doctors, who have been hanged in a square in Aleppo, Syria, in 1916, during the Armenian genocide.

culture. It deported Armenians in cattle cars and sunk barges filled with Armenian refugees on the Black Sea.

The duty of the SO was the formation of killing squads not unlike the Einsatzgruppen, or mobile killing units, that Germany was to employ twenty years later for the roundup and execution of Jews and other groups that had been declared enemies of the Nazi regime. In Turkey, the killing squads were commanded by military officers but were made up of ex-convicts (many released from prisons expressly for this purpose), outlaws and ruffians, and Kurdish tribesmen. Known as *chetes*, these killer bands were motivated by the principle of jihad, or holy war against nonbelievers of Islam.

Arrests and deportations of Armenian citizens were also carried out by military police known as *gendarmes*, who had local and provincial jurisdiction. These officers might be compared to the Gestapo of Hitler's Germany, who conducted searches within the community for people attempting to hide themselves or their possessions from the authorities.

As the World Looked On

Although the United States did not enter World War I until 1917, no other nation was more aware of the ongoing atrocities of the Armenian genocide or more closely concerned with rescue and relief efforts. Reports by American missionaries, church personnel, medical workers, educators, and general observers; by American consuls in Turkish cities; and by Morgenthau all revealed the extent and the cruelty of the genocide.

In addition to the killings, both immediate and extended, the Turkish government used torture. The bastinado, a form of punishment inflicted by beating the soles of the feet with a thin rod, was only one of several methods employed. Prisoners' hairs were pulled out one by one, their fingernails and toenails were extracted, and their hands and feet were nailed to pieces of wood in a mocking reminder of the crucifixion of Christ.

By October 1915, relief funds from churches, the Rockefeller Foundation, the Committee on Armenian Atrocities, and other private groups began pouring into the country.

In 1917, President Woodrow Wilson finally declared war, but only against two nations: Germany and Austria. He refused to declare war on Turkey. Like so many American heads of state who followed him, he was reluctant to expand the war effort and felt that the offer of humanitarian aid to victims of the genocide was sufficient.

When the war ended in November 1918 with an Allied victory, it was Great Britain, followed by France and Russia, that led the demand for tribunals to punish the guilty members of the Turkish leadership for crimes against humanity. The United States did not take part. Prosecutions led to a handful of death sentences. Other guilty parties received jail sentences with hard labor.

Among the relatively few perpetrators of the genocide from whom retribution was exacted was Mehmet Talaat, or Talaat Pasha, a member of the Young Turk triumvirate. Along with many other high-ranking officials, Talaat had been given asylum in Germany, where he was living incognito. On March 14, 1921, Talaat was shot to death on a Berlin street by a twenty-four-year-old Armenian genocide survivor, Soghomon Tehlirian. In 1915, Tehlirian had been part of a deportation march during which his sisters had been sexually assaulted, his brother's head had been split open with an axe, and his mother had been shot. After a blow on the head rendered him unconscious, Tehlirian awoke amidst a pile of corpses. His entire family was gone.

"This is to avenge the death of my family!" the young man cried as he placed the pistol against Talaat's head and pulled the trigger. At Tehlirian's trial later that year, he was acquitted of murder on the grounds of temporary insanity and lived the rest of his life in California.

The present-day Republic of Turkey continues to deny that any genocide of the Armenian people took place. It argues that Armenians were caught in the crossfire during a time of chaos and war and insists that the death toll has been blown out of proportion.

In 1918, the country of Armenia emerged as independent from Turkey as World War I drew to a close. Three years later, it was integrated into the Soviet Union. With that nation crumbling in 1991, Armenia seceded. Today, Armenia maintains strained relations with its neighbor, Turkey, in large part because of Turkish officials' denial of the genocide.

Chapter Three

THE HOLOCAUST

The Armenians of Turkey and the Jews of Germany were both adherents of an ancient religion and had experienced a long history of persecution. Both were religious minorities in their respective countries. Neither had a homeland of their own, and each would later seek to build a new nation that could be home to the survivors of genocide.

The similarities between the crimes suffered by these two persecuted peoples do not stop there. Jews of German-ruled Europe were ordered, as Nazi power grew and advanced across national borders, to identify themselves by wearing a Star of David drawn on yellow cloth pinned to their outer clothing. The six-pointed star, a sacred religious symbol that Hitler chose as a "badge of shame" to set

Opposite: During an uprising in the ghetto in Warsaw, Poland, in 1943, Jews are led away by Nazi soldiers for deportation.

the Jews apart, was only one of many such markers. Throughout the Jews' long history, anti-Semitic regimes had required the wearing of other such badges, as well as garments of various colors and design.

Similarly, the Armenians, who for centuries lived as subjects of the Ottoman Empire, had been obliged to wear certain colors and styles of clothing that would distinguish them from the Muslim majority. At one time they were forbidden to dress in silk, furs, and other valuable materials and were not allowed to wear turbans.

In the end, just as Nazi leader Adolf Hitler's plans for ethnic cleansing drew strength from the mass murder of Native Americans, so too did Hitler find sinister inspiration in the Armenian genocide. In 1939, days before Hitler's September 1 invasion of Poland and the start of World War II, his instructions to his killing squads were to show no mercy in their genocidal acts. "Who today, after all," Hitler queried, "speaks of the annihilation of the Armenians?"

The Rise of Hitler and the Nazis

World War I ended in 1918 with the victory of Britain, France, Russia, and the United States over Germany and its Austrian and Turkish allies. An estimated ten million military personnel had died. Ironically, the "war to end all wars," as it was popularly called in its day, laid the groundwork for World War II, which was to break out in 1939.

The peace terms dictated by the victors in 1918 were punishing. Germany was forced to disarm, give up territory, and pay reparations. A severe economic depression ensued, and in 1933, the Austrian-born dictator-to-be Adolf Hitler rose to power.

Vowing to rearm Germany and restore its honor, the violently anti-Semitic leader of the National Socialist, or Nazi, Party

German führer (leader) Adolf Hitler speaks at a rally. Hitler sparked World War II and led a murderous campaign throughout Europe.

crushed all political opposition and instituted laws that deprived Germany's Jews of their rights as citizens. At the same time, he built a vast propaganda and law-enforcement machine, ranging from the Hitler Youth groups to the Gestapo spy agency and the murderous Einsatzgruppen, or mobile killing squads.

Hitler's assault on Jews began in 1933, when he ordered all Germans to boycott Jewish shops and businesses, ensuring that they would be forced to close. Jewish children were banned from attending German schools; Jewish doctors, educators, and other professionals were forbidden to practice; and Jews had to have their papers stamped with an identifying "J." Little overt opposition to Hitler's anti-Jewish policies sprang up. The emotions of the non-Jewish German population ranged from fear of retribution to enthusiastic support.

The violent government-backed attacks on Jewish synagogues, schools, hospitals, orphanages, and homes on November 9–10, 1938, signaled the beginning of open warfare against those Jews who had not yet fled Germany. Mobs smashed, shattered, burned, and looted Jewish property during what was known as Kristallnacht—the Night of Broken Glass.

The arrest of Jews had by that point become widespread, the victims taken without warrants or other official documents to labor and concentration camps within Germany, among them Dachau and Buchenwald. The two camps were the first to have been built for the express purpose of incarcerating Jews and others seen as enemies of the regime. There, people languished while anxious families besieged the offices of the Gestapo, or secret police, for news of their loved ones.

The Genocidal Campaign Expands

For Hitler, the cleansing of Germany to make it *Judenrein*—free of Jews—was only the beginning of the changes he sought to make. He was determined to take control of more of Europe than Germany had ever possessed. For a time, he succeeded, seizing Austria and Czechoslovakia in 1938; Poland in 1939; and Denmark, Norway, Belgium, Luxembourg, the Netherlands, and France in 1940.

In all of these countries, Jews, Romany (commonly known as Gypsies), communists, and dissidents were slated for imprisonment and extermination. New concentration camps were built, ranging from Westerbork in the Netherlands—a holding and transit camp for Jews—to the dreaded Auschwitz/Birkenau complex and other death camps in Poland.

Meanwhile, the slaughter of Poland's more than three million Jews could not proceed fast enough for the Nazi killing machine.

Gas chambers and cremation ovens designed for murdering large numbers of people at once were still in the process of being built, so the Nazis sent their mobile squads, the Einsatzgruppen, into the cities and towns of both Poland and neighboring Lithuania.

In the summer of 1941, an underground Polish organization known as the Jewish Labor Bund reported:

> *Men, fourteen to sixty years old, were driven to a single place, a square or a cemetery, where they were slaughtered or shot by machine guns or killed by hand grenades. They had to dig their own graves. Children in orphanages, inmates in old-age homes, the sick in hospitals were shot, women were killed in the streets. In many towns, Jews were carried off to an "unknown destination" and killed in adjacent woods.*

Prior to the completion of the gas chambers in the death camps, the Nazis gassed one thousand Polish Jews per day by cramming as many as ninety at a time into mobile gas vans. Before the corpses were buried or burned, gold rings, gold teeth, hair, and clothing were salvaged and sent back to Germany.

International Awareness Grows

Reports of the killings in Poland were received and released by Szmul Zygielbojm, a Polish Jew who made them public on the BBC in London in June 1942. As the situation worsened, Zygielbojm pleaded with American officials (the United States had entered the war in December 1941) on behalf of the Polish government-in-exile to bomb the rail lines to the death camps.

Zygielbojm, however, was told that not enough aircraft were available for that purpose. When he learned that his wife and child had died in the embattled Warsaw ghetto, Zygielbojm took an overdose of sleeping pills on May 12, 1943. In his suicide note, Zygielbojm wrote that the "crime of murdering the entire Jewish population of Poland falls ... on the perpetrators ... but indirectly also it weighs on the whole of humanity." The *New York Times* published Zygielbojm's despairing letter in its entirety on June 4, 1943, under the headline "Pole's Suicide Note Pleads for Jews."

Another voice aimed at persuading the United States to take action against the wholesale killing of Jews in eastern Europe was that of Jan Karski. In 1942, Karski, a young Polish diplomat and a Roman Catholic, entered the Warsaw ghetto disguised as a Jew and was able to report on the walled-in fortress that contained five hundred thousand Jews trying to hold out against German might. Karski had also been successful in infiltrating a sorting station for the Nazi death camp of Belzec, near the Polish border with Ukraine.

Carrying microfilmed documents testifying to the horrors he had witnessed, Karski made his way to the United States and met with Supreme Court justice Felix Frankfurter, himself a Jew of German background. Frankfurter's response after listening carefully to Karski was, "I don't believe you ... I do not mean that you are lying. I simply said I cannot believe you."

Disbelief regarding the emaciated occupants of the Warsaw ghetto and the victims of the Belzec death camp would be understandable had the evidence come from a solitary witness. But there were also the reports of Zygielbojm and the Jewish Labor Bund. By 1942, seven hundred thousand Jews had already been killed in Poland alone. Throughout Europe, one million more had been murdered. The *New York Times* picked up the Jewish Labor Bund's story that year, but it was buried in one of the back pages of the newspaper.

In the end, the war strategy of the Allied nations—Britain, Russia, and the United States—was to defeat Germany militarily and to worry about its crimes against humanity later. Victory came at last in 1945, when many Americans for the first time saw the horrors inside the Nazi concentration camps: countless starving and emaciated prisoners and piles of bodies put to death in gas chambers. The controversy over how much the Allies knew about German concentration camps, when they knew it, and what they should have done about it continues to this day. It must be acknowledged that anti-Semitism was ingrained in the culture of all of the fighting nations; this cultural and religious prejudice had existed in many parts of the world since before the first Jewish exile from Palestine, as early as the sixth century BCE.

Giving Genocide a Name

Soghomon Tehlirian's 1921 assassination of Talaat Pasha, one of the powerful Turkish leaders behind the Armenian genocide, drew the attention of Raphael Lemkin, a twenty-one-year-old Polish Jew. Lemkin was at the time studying linguistics at the University of Lvov in Poland. He found himself questioning Tehlirian's arrest for the crime. If it was illegal to kill one person, how great was the illegality of killing one million? Did a sovereign state have the freedom to murder beyond limits, although individuals did not?

Raphael Lemkin, a lawyer and a Polish Jew, gave the name "genocide" to the atrocities committed during the Holocaust.

By 1933, having attained a law degree, Lemkin found himself

an early victim of Hitler's influence on neighboring Poland. He had wanted to present a paper he had written that called attention to the Turkish ethnic cleansing of the Armenians at an international law conference in Madrid, Spain. The Polish government, however, refused to let him leave the country.

His paper condemned the "Barbarity" of "the premeditated destruction of national, racial, religious, and social collectivities." Lemkin called attention to "the destruction of works of art and culture, being the expression of the particular genius of these collectivities." Lemkin also warned of the dangers of Hitler's ascent to power. As a result, the anti-Semitic Warsaw government fired him from his job as deputy public prosecutor.

Hitler's invasion of Poland on September 1, 1939, was the signal for Lemkin to flee. He managed to find refuge in Sweden in early 1940 and to reach the United States in April 1941. Like Zygielbojm and Karski, Lemkin tried to contact officials in the highest government offices to persuade them to take action against the barbarities being enacted in Nazi-held Europe.

He lobbied for a treaty making the protection of minorities one of the aims of the war against Germany, but his efforts met with no interest from either President Franklin Roosevelt or his vice president, Henry Wallace. Roosevelt refused him an audience and sent Lemkin a message advising patience.

On May 8, 1945, World War II ended. Six million Jews and five million Poles, Romany, communists, homosexuals, and other "undesirables" had been killed because of their ethnic, racial, sexual, or religious identities. By this time, Lemkin had at last coined a term that could describe the barbarity that had taken place: genocide.

Lemkin hoped that the Nuremberg Trials of 1945, in which Germany was prosecuted for its crimes against humanity, would be the venue for the formulation of an international agreement leading to both the condemnation of and action against guilty nations. However, disappointingly, the Nuremberg tribunal did not take into account Hitler's crimes against Germany's Jews before the war because at that time Germany had been a sovereign state. Only Hitler's crimes in the conquered territories were placed under investigation.

Lemkin nonetheless persevered. A new international organization, the United Nations, had been founded in San Francisco in 1945. In 1946, the fledgling alliance of countries met on Long Island in New York, and Lemkin was there, determined to introduce a resolution for a law that called for international action against the crime of genocide.

Lemkin succeeded in spurring the United Nations to form a subcommittee to examine and define the crime of genocide and to make it punishable under international law. The UN Convention on the Prevention and Punishment of the Crime of Genocide (CPPCG) met in Geneva, Switzerland, in 1948, and Lemkin attended to lobby the delegates of the various nations represented and to urge its ratification.

Lemkin had learned since the end of the war that close to fifty members of his family had perished, most of them in the Warsaw ghetto, in the concentration camps, or on death marches. Of his immediate family, only his older brother had survived. It was vital to Lemkin that the definition of genocide on which the CPPCG agreed should cover as many aspects as possible of this crime. The convention was approved and adopted in 1948.

Ratification of the resolution on genocide by the delegates to the subcommittee and by a number of UN member states took place readily. In June 1949, President Harry Truman called for its ratification by the US Senate, where a two-thirds vote was required for adoption. To the despair of Raphael Lemkin and many others, objections began to be raised.

How many individuals of a specific group had to be killed to call a situation genocide? What if it was only a very small number?

The International Definition of Genocide

The definition of "genocide" agreed upon by the United Nations in 1948 was as follows: "genocide means any of the following acts committed with intent to destroy, in whole or in part, a national, ethnical, racial, or religious group, as such:

- Killing members of the group;
- Causing serious bodily or mental harm to members of the group;
- Deliberately inflicting on the group the conditions of life calculated to bring about its physical destruction in whole or in part;
- Imposing measures intended to prevent births within the group;
- Forcibly transferring children of the group to another group."

During times of peace or war, national leaders, public officials, and even private citizens are liable for punishment if they commit crimes that fall under the definition above. Attacks on untargeted groups with no special identification are not considered genocide; they are defined as mass homicide and do not fall under the aegis of the United Nations' CPPCG.

Would the treatment of American Indians and African Americans by the United States be considered genocide? Would punishment be retroactive? Should a powerful nation such as the United States allow international law to infringe on its sovereignty? Was the United States open to the idea of responding to charges brought by other nations regarding its infractions? Hardly.

Under Truman's 1953 successor, Dwight D. Eisenhower, the battle for ratification died. Even though the troops commanded by this former World War II general had liberated Germany's Buchenwald concentration camp, the self-protective legal interests of the United States remained foremost.

In 1959, a despairing Lemkin succumbed to a heart attack. He had received a number of nominations for the Nobel Peace Prize but never received it. It would not be until 1988 that the United States would finally ratify the UN treaty on the crime that Raphael Lemkin named.

The Holocaust remains the most notorious and widely known genocide in history. Its ripple effects continue to this day all over the globe and especially in the nation of Israel, which was founded as a Jewish homeland after World War II ended. The world could no longer ignore the horrors of such crimes—instead, world leaders decided, something had to be done should a genocide ever occur again. How, exactly, the international community should respond, however, remained unclear.

Chapter Four

THE KILLING FIELDS OF CAMBODIA

The swift cultural, political, and genocidal revolution that took hold of the Southeast Asian country of Cambodia in April 1975 was, like the genocides of the Armenians, Jews, and Native Americans, fueled by religious and class-related divisions. In just over three years, it claimed the lives of an estimated 25 percent of the Cambodian population and left a country scarred, with no family untouched by terrible loss.

The Influence of Communism

Also like the Armenian genocide and the Holocaust, the Cambodian genocide took place in the context

Opposite: The remains of those who were murdered in the killing fields of Phnom Penh are pictured here in 1981 and can still be seen there today.

of a major war. Since 1959, the United States had been involved in a war against Communist North Vietnam in support of non-Communist South Vietnam. Fighting had overflowed into neighboring Cambodia.

In 1975, the United States withdrew from Vietnam in defeat; the Communists had won. As a result, Lon Nol, the corrupt and repressive anti-Communist head of state of Cambodia whom the Americans had been backing, also fled.

This turn of events gave the Khmer Rouge ("Red Cambodians") the opportunity to take control of Cambodia. Their leaders had been schooled in the extremist Communist ideology of Mao Zedong, a founder of the Chinese Communist Party and former leader of the People's Republic of China. Mao's theories reinterpreted those of Communism's founders—Karl Marx and Vladimir Lenin—to elevate the importance of the peasantry—that is, the masses of food-growers and laborers who formed the basis of society. China was ideologically but not militarily involved in the Khmer Rouge takeover.

During the Cultural Revolution, which peaked in 1966–1969 in China, Communist leader Mao Zedong attempted to bring back the "classless" society of the early days of the revolution. He placed authority in the hands of a group of young soldiers known as the Red Guards. The Red Guards were empowered to denounce and attack intellectuals, university professors, scientists, artists, and anyone else they decided to label a "class enemy." Universities were closed, and foreign culture was banned. Public ridicule of the accused led to suicides. Jailing and constant hounding led to thousands of deaths.

It was from this aspect of Maoist thought that the Khmer Rouge drew their ideas for the governance of Cambodia. The Khmer Kingdom, a nineteenth-century protectorate of France that was once a powerful empire and most recently a wartime enemy of the United States, was about to experience one of the most vicious assaults on humanity that the world had ever seen. Under the new name Democratic Kampuchea, between 1.7 and 2 million people (and by some estimates, up to 3 million) would be shot, bludgeoned, tortured, and worked and starved to death within the space of three and a half years, mainly for cultural and political reasons, but also for their religious adherence to Islam, Buddhism, or Christianity.

Who Were the Khmer Rouge?

Reviewing the unbridled barbarism of the killings in Cambodia, the following question has been asked by historians and other observers: Would the Khmer Rouge have been so brutal in their attack on society if the American bombings of the preceding years had not been so intense? The more than 500,000 tons (453,592 metric tons) of bombs dropped on Cambodia by the anti-Communist United States was three times greater than what had been dropped on Japan in World War II, including the two atom bombs. The bombings reportedly inspired many Cambodians to join the Communist resistance that would become the Khmer Rouge.

Most of those who joined had been recruited from the poorest regions of the countryside, where they lived without running water or electricity, without schools, without money, without automotive vehicles or even roads. Under the tutelage of the Khmer leaders, they had learned to despise the cities, especially the sophisticated capital of Phnom Penh, where intellectuals, educators, and wealthy businessmen lived. They were taught to view the cities as evil places where capitalism thrived.

The Evacuation of Phnom Penh

The Khmer Rouge's initial orders that day in April were that Phnom Penh be evacuated. On entering the homes of the city dwellers forced to leave at gunpoint, the Khmer recruits were astonished by refrigerators and modern sanitary equipment. "Soldiers drank water from toilet bowls, thinking they were what city people used instead of wells … others ate toothpaste."

They vandalized furnishings; commandeered motorbikes and automobiles, which they promptly drove into trees or buildings; broke into shops; and destroyed property. Many of the newly recruited troops were teenagers, even children of eleven or twelve, armed with AK-47 machine guns.

However, the material destruction in the city was nothing compared with the fate that awaited the city dwellers. On the afternoon of April 17, the inhabitants were told that the Americans were about to bomb the city and that they would be able to return in two or three days. This was untrue. Nevertheless, some six hundred thousand longtime city dwellers, as well as about two million refugees from the American bombing, found themselves on the crowded roads heading north out of the capital.

"It was a stupefying sight, a human flood pouring out of the city … bicycles overflowing with bundles, and others behind little home-made carts. Most were on foot." The Khmer Rouge ordered the city's hospitals, housing fifteen to twenty thousand people at the time, to be emptied immediately. "Sick people were left by their families at the roadside. Others were killed [by the soldiers] because they could walk no further. Children who had lost their parents cried out in tears … The dead were abandoned, covered in flies, sometimes with a piece of cloth thrown over them. Women gave birth wherever they could."

The leader who was to take control of Cambodia after April 1975 and direct the murderous regime to follow was a little-known member of the Communist Party of Kampuchea (CPK) and a former schoolteacher by the name of Saloth Sar. Believing that disguise was the best protection against one's enemies, Saloth Sar had many aliases. The name that would make him as notorious and universally despised as Adolf Hitler was Pol Pot.

Pol Pot's Rise to Power

Unlike most Khmer Rouge soldiers, the man eventually known as Pol Pot was born the son of a relatively prosperous rice farmer in 1925. Like his brothers, Saloth Sar was educated, first at a Buddhist monastery for a year and then at a school run by French Catholic priests in Phnom Penh. Later, he was awarded a scholarship to an engineering school in France.

Arriving in Paris in 1949, Saloth Sar underwent a political transformation. He joined a movement to free Cambodia from

Deposed Cambodian dictator Pol Pot is pictured in 1979 in a guerrilla base on the border between Cambodia and Thailand.

French control and to rid it of its ruler, Prince Norodom Sihanouk. He joined the French Communist Party. He saw the abolition of private property and the creation of an egalitarian society as his true revolutionary goal for Cambodia.

Saloth Sar returned to Cambodia in 1953 and joined a Vietnamese Communist guerrilla base camp in the Cambodian forest east of Phnom Penh. In 1963, he went into hiding in the jungle, where he would direct military operations against the government and bide his time. In 1966, when the Cultural Revolution erupted in China, Saloth Sar declared, "organisationally and ideologically our people are ready ... to launch a true people's war," and he hailed Mao Zedong as "the great, guiding star who brings unceasing victories."

The monarchy was overthrown in 1970, so after the hurried departure of the Americans in 1975, the time was finally ripe for Saloth Sar and his associates to strike. The American bombing had killed five hundred thousand Cambodians; Pol Pot would murder millions.

Life in the Communes

Bewildered evacuees driven out of Phnom Penh and other cities, bearing little more than the few possessions they could wheel or carry, were told they were headed for safety. Their destinations were actually the various zones throughout the country where rural life predominated and where rice growing was the main occupation.

In these agricultural areas, private property and ownership of material goods would not exist. The national goal set by Pol Pot and members of the CPK was increased farm production. To this end, the "new" people arriving from the cities (some six hundred thousand from Phnom Penh alone) were required to join the "old" or "base" people native to the region in laboring long

Cambodian citizens are forced to work on an irrigation project near the Chinith River in 1976.

hours in the rice fields, not only to grow rice but to dig irrigation ditches that were intended to increase the harvests.

Life as the new people had known it was stripped down to its barest essentials. They lived and ate in communes under the watchful eyes of Khmer Rouge village militias, which included both men and women. Like their overseers, the new people wore black, but they were permitted no colorful scarves or other adornments; no watches, radios, cameras, books, or currency. Former doctors, lawyers, educators, university students, civil servants, and even persons who wore eyeglasses, and were thus considered intellectuals, were put under constant surveillance for remarks or behavior disloyal to Angkar, the faceless leadership that ran Democratic Kampuchea.

"Angkar" can be loosely translated as "the Organization" or "Big Brother." At the lowest levels, Angkar (not to be confused with Angkor Wat, the richly carved temple of the ancient Khmer Empire in northwestern Cambodia) was the village committee that held autonomy over the lives of the recently arrived rice-field laborers and could order an on-the-spot execution with the blow of an axe or a hoe handle at any time. At the highest levels, Angkar was Pol Pot and the other national leaders.

The overseers of the communes varied in the severity of the punishments they doled out. Some were stony-faced, others capricious and unpredictable. Most were illiterate and predisposed toward anger at the former city dwellers. A frequently punished crime was the search for food to supplement the minimal daily ration of rice. People who were caught eating grass, crickets, grasshoppers, snails, frogs, snakes, and rats to supplement their near-starvation diets were liable to be put to death.

Starvation was a major cause of natural death, as were diseases such as malaria and dysentery. Modern medicine was abandoned, and those unable to work were neither treated nor fed. The work week, as it was in the days of the French Revolution, consisted of ten days, followed by one day off.

Angkar abolished the concept of paying wages, along with money and markets for the purpose of purchasing food, clothing, and other necessities. Food, clothing, and shelter were supplied by the state, which was, in effect, a slave state, in which human beings were viewed as little more than oxen.

When a person was to be killed for violating the rules of the commune, the view of local leaders was: "To keep you is no profit, to destroy you is no loss." People could also be killed for confessing to past sins, such as loyalty to the former Cambodian regime; a suspect from the cities who did so could be sent away for "reeducation," never to reappear. In the worst of the atrocities committed, local leaders might slit open the belly of a pregnant woman and remove her fetus or extract the liver of an executed person for use as human food. The Khmer Rouge's various forms of cultural, class, and religious genocide showed an overarching indifference to human life.

Family life was also sacrificed to Angkar. Starting in the summer of 1976, children were taken away from their parents at the age of seven so that they could be indoctrinated into the teachings of the revolution and sent to work in the fields. Schools for elementary learning had been abolished.

Spouses, too, were often separated and sent to different areas of the country to work. Marriage and the birth of children, however, were encouraged in order to increase the labor supply. Existing marriages were sometimes ignored by the authorities; instead, Angkar selected the mates and conducted the marriages, usually of ten or fifteen couples at one time.

The Killing Fields

Where did people go when they were sent off for "reeducation"? And who was most likely to be sent there?

While the genocide inflicted by Pol Pot and his comrades can be seen as the destruction of one segment of Cambodian culture by another, there were also groups within Cambodia that were targeted because of their religion. Buddhist and Catholic books were burned in Phnom Penh, and the practice of both religions was prohibited. Cambodian Muslims, known as Chams, after the eastern region of Cambodia that many inhabited, were forbidden to wear Islamic dress, keep their own customs, marry among themselves, and worship in their mosques. Khmer policy broke down the cultural solidarity of the Cham Muslims by dispersing them throughout the countryside.

In sum, the Khmer Rouge had a broad definition of who was not considered "pure." Everyone from intellectuals to Muslims, from Buddhists to Vietnamese minorities, had to be "cleansed." When they were sent off for "reeducation," they were often tortured and killed, forced to dig their own shallow graves before they were executed, often by a blow to the head. They were buried in mass graves in rural areas—what have become known as the "killing fields." A total of 19,733 mass graves at more than 388 locations around the country have been identified to date.

Consolidating Power

Aside from Pol Pot's contacts with the Chinese Communist hierarchy, Cambodia had become a closed-off nation operating behind a wall of silence. There were no news reports, no foreign communications, and no flights into or out of the country. In keeping with his penchant for secrecy, Pol Pot did not even take the title of prime minister until 1976, after Prince Sihanouk, horrified by the Khmer Rouge regime, abdicated in April of that year.

Within a twelve- to eighteen-month period, Pol Pot believed he had created the ideal Communist state. He boasted that the CPK had achieved a new and better form of Communism than that of other totalitarian nations, one that would make Kampuchea strong and preserve it forever. Its hardworking peasant class was becoming the foundation of the national economy—selfless, productive, and pledged to the ideology of the Khmer Rouge leaders.

Pol Pot, however, would grow suspicious of the loyalty and ambitious motives of his comrades and fellow leaders, resulting in widespread purges beginning in early 1976. For the purpose of extracting confessions from this group of mainly upper-echelon political prisoners, he set up interrogation centers around the country. The largest of these was located in an abandoned high school in Phnom Penh and was known as Tuol Sleng, code-named S-21.

The Khmer Rouge Collapses

Throughout 1977, operations at Tuol Sleng continued unrelentingly, stripping Pol Pot's government of many officials in the top ranks of the CPK. Regional and local leaders, too, went to their deaths after numerous forced confessions, which took place at interrogation centers located around the country. As a result, leaders on all levels had to be shifted around or replaced with increasing frequency.

In an effort to save the failing system that the Khmer Rouge had established in 1975, in 1978, Pol Pot began to allow a few more individual freedoms. Individual cooking, as opposed to compulsory communal meals, was permitted, and people who foraged for frogs, snakes, and other field animals to supplement their near-starvation rice diets were not punished with death. For the first time, "new" people and "old" or "base" people were permitted to intermarry and children were given basic elementary schooling in some localities. The Khmer Rouge even permitted the first American journalists to enter the country since the evacuation of Phnom Penh.

Fear and loathing of the Communist Vietnamese had been building among the Khmer Rouge for some years. Border skirmishes between the two countries increased during 1978, and Vietnam set up training camps for Khmer refugees. On December 25, 1978, the Vietnamese launched a full-fledged attack, sending 120,000 well-armed troops into southeastern Cambodia. By January 7, 1979, Vietnam had taken Phnom Penh.

After seeing that all remaining prisoners at Tuol Sleng were exterminated, Pol Pot fled to Thailand by helicopter. There had been no time, however, to destroy the archives of the deadly interrogation center.

The Tuol Sleng Torture Center

There were indications early on that the revolution was not producing enough Communist zeal or increasing rice production in the way that Pol Pot had hoped. So Pol Pot began to round up political personnel with the aim of extracting confessions of wrongdoing, punishable by death. Tuol Sleng "processed" sixteen thousand people, of which only a handful survived.

Chances of release were almost nil because condemnation came without proof. Prisoners were tortured with electric shocks, seared with hot metal rods, beaten on the soles of their feet, and suspended from hooks with their heads submerged in water. The orders were that as many confessions as possible must be obtained before executions were to take place.

Khmer Rouge authorities were seeking to root out people with connections to such hostile nations as the United States, the Soviet Union, and Vietnam. Although the Communist Vietnamese who had infiltrated Cambodia in the early days had nurtured the growth of that country's Communist movement, Pol Pot now repudiated their influence. He had become paranoid and hostile toward Cambodia's neighbor to the east. The behavior of Pol Pot in purging his corevolutionists was similar to that of Soviet leader Joseph Stalin.

Tuol Sleng prisoners who were tortured to the point of confessing membership in the KGB, the Soviet Union's spy organization, were doomed to die. Many were also forced to falsely name other guilty parties. The Soviets were seen as enemies of the Chinese, who had supported the Cambodian revolutionists. Forced confessions

A shackle lies on the floor of a small cell in the Tuol Sleng prison, where thousands of people were tortured and killed.

of working for the CIA, the American spy organization, also merited a death sentence.

The confession files of the Tuol Sleng prisoners have been preserved, as have some five thousand photographs of innocent men, women, and children arriving at what was to be their final destination. Their portraits can still be seen at the Tuol Sleng Genocide Museum in Phnom Penh.

For a decade, Pol Pot hovered in the jungle wilderness near Cambodia's northern border with Thailand, hoping to gather sufficient military strength to drive the Vietnamese out of the country. Meanwhile, Khmer Rouge refugees, having renounced their Cambodian Communist Party affiliation, formed a coalition government with the occupying Vietnamese.

At last, the wall of silence that had encircled Cambodia between 1975 and early 1979 had been breached. The international community was shocked at the mass graves of the Cambodian killing fields—giant earthen saucers from which huge quantities of bones and skulls protruded.

Seeking Justice on the International Stage

A memorandum sent to US president Gerald Ford in 1976 detailed many of the atrocities and widespread executions taking place in Cambodia. Yet despite publicly denouncing the actions of the Khmer Rouge, the United States did not intervene.

Still smarting from its defeat in Vietnam and opposed to that nation's legitimacy on the international stage, the United States supported the claim of the vastly reduced Khmer Rouge government to maintain its seat in the United Nations, even after the taking of Phnom Penh revealed the extent of the atrocities it had committed. Meanwhile, UN member states that had signed the treaty calling for the Prevention and Punishment of the Crime of Genocide did not file charges against the Khmer Rouge at the International Court of Justice. The member states simply looked the other way in spite of a UN final report that condemned Cambodia's crimes as "the most serious that had occurred anywhere in the world since Nazism."

Many Khmer Rouge leaders escaped punishment. Pol Pot, principal among them, was never brought to trial. He died of a

Nuon Chea, a high-ranking Khmer Rouge official, is on trial in 2011. He was found guilty of genocide and crimes against humanity.

heart attack in April 1998. The Cambodian people would see few attempts at justice until eight years later.

In 2001, the Cambodian National Assembly founded the Extraordinary Chambers in the Courts of Cambodia with assistance from the United Nations. To date, nine cases have been brought before the ECCC, with three convictions. The United States Holocaust Memorial Museum writes that this tribunal "reflects a strengthening global consensus that, no matter how much time has passed, perpetrators of the modern era's worst crimes must be brought to account, in a framework that helps survivors repair their lives."

Chapter Five

THE GENOCIDE IN RWANDA

"I had accepted death," recalls Rwandan lawyer Laurent Nkongoli of the genocide that ravaged his country in 1994. "At a certain moment this happens. One hopes not to die cruelly, but one expects to die anyway. Not death by machete, one hopes, but with a bullet. If you were willing to pay for it, you could often ask for a bullet."

In the tiny east-central African nation of Rwanda, during a period of just one hundred days in the spring and summer of 1994, an estimated eight hundred thousand people were murdered. One-tenth of the country's total population was shot, blown up with grenades, or hacked to death with machetes, knives, bamboo spears, or the traditional Rwandan masu—a club from which

Opposite: Refugees of the Rwandan genocide travel toward the border with Zaire, seeking to escape the violence.

nails protrude. When these weapons were not available, the killers used "screwdrivers, hammers, and bicycle handlebars." They even made knives out of the sharpened leaf springs of demolished automobiles.

The international community did not intervene in these brutal killings. Afterwards, many—including US president Bill Clinton—expressed regret that they did not do more. To understand how this genocide took place and why no one intervened, we must first learn more about the Rwandan people.

The Hutu and the Tutsi

Who were the killers, who were the victims, and what was the root cause of the genocide that flared up in Rwanda? In the sixteenth century, the Hutu of the region, a Bantu people who inhabited much of central and southern Africa, were invaded by the Tutsi, a northern people said to have originated in Ethiopia.

Soon the Hutu, who were in the majority, were being ruled by a series of Tutsi kings known as *mwamis*. While the Hutu were farmers, the Tutsi were herdsmen, many made wealthy and powerful through their ownership of cattle. There were said to be differences, too, in the physical features of the two groups. The Hutu, for example, were believed to be darker-skinned than the Tutsi.

The two groups spoke the same language, were followers of the same religion, and intermarried so that over time the so-called distinct physical features had begun to merge.

From the late 1800s until just after World War I, present-day Rwanda was part of German East Africa. Following Germany's defeat in the war, the colony was mandated to Belgium, which became its next colonial overseer. Although the Tutsi kings continued to rule, the Belgians saw fit in the 1930s to issue ethnic identity cards, distinguishing Tutsis from Hutus. The purpose appeared to be mainly administrative.

In 1959, the Hutu majority supported a dictatorial Hutu president and deposed the Tutsi rulers. More change came with the abolition of the Rwandan monarchy in 1961 and Rwandan independence from Belgium in 1962. As a result, 150,000 Tutsi fled to the small neighboring nation of Burundi, where a Tutsi military regime was in place. Most Tutsis, however, remained in Rwanda.

Hutu majority rule offered long-sought satisfaction to the nearly 85 percent of the population that had once been ruled by Tutsi kings. In the new republic, however, there was to be a power-sharing arrangement, which would permit both groups to live in harmony. However, peaceful relations between them had not existed for three decades. By 1990, refugee Tutsis in neighboring Uganda had formed the Rwandan Patriotic Front (RPF) and were making sporadic attacks on Hutus in Rwanda. Meanwhile, Hutu Youth militias and the Hutu Power movement within Rwanda were training for war and stockpiling weapons.

In 1993, concerned western powers and the African country of Tanzania initiated peace talks in the Tanzanian city of Arusha. Under the so-called Arusha Accords, Rwanda's leaders agreed that moderate Hutu parties and Tutsi opposition parties would both participate in the government. There would also be a peace agreement between the Hutu president, Juvénal Habyarimana, and the Tutsi RPF.

To preside over the peace agreement, the United Nations sent a peacekeeping force to Rwanda to patrol the cease-fire. The multinational UN Assistance Mission in Rwanda (UNAMIR) was under the command of a Canadian military officer, Lieutenant General Roméo Dallaire. UNAMIR's assignment did not permit the discharge of arms unless its members were directly attacked.

Nevertheless, it was felt that the presence of 2,500 blue-helmeted UN soldiers from Belgium, Bangladesh, Ghana, Tunisia, and twenty other countries would prove effective in preserving the goals of the Arusha Accords. This proved not to be the case.

The Violence Begins

As soon as Lieutenant General Dallaire and his UNAMIR force arrived in Rwanda late in 1993, the commander became aware of how little attention was being paid to the high-minded Arusha Accords. Through a secret informant he learned that Hutu Power extremists had drawn up lists of Tutsis living in the Rwandan capital of Kigali whom they planned to slay.

In addition, the Hutu, who had been importing guns from France and machetes from China, had major arms caches hidden throughout the country. It seemed the Hutu were also planning to murder as many of the 440 Belgian peacekeepers as possible in order to drive them out of Rwanda. Nor was the rest of UNAMIR welcome in Hutu-controlled Rwanda. The peacekeeping force was seen as an accomplice of the Tutsi minority.

Dallaire was petitioning the United Nations for more and better-supplied peacekeepers and for permission to perform arms sweeps in Rwanda when the event that catalyzed the genocide took place. On April 6, 1994, the private jet of Hutu president Habyarimana, who was returning from a meeting in Tanzania, was shot down by ground-fired missiles as it approached the Kigali airport. In the plane along with Habyarimana were several high-level aides and the recently elected president of Burundi, Cyprien Ntaryamira. All those aboard were killed.

The question of who was responsible for the president's murder would never be fully resolved. Were those who downed the plane Hutu extremists or Tutsi oppositionists? As events unfolded, it appeared more and more likely that the attackers had been hard-line Hutus seeking license to begin the bloody elimination of moderate Hutus (those who favored power-sharing) and of all Tutsis in Rwanda.

Among the very first victims of the genocide killed on April 7 was the prime minister of Rwanda, Agathe Uwilingiyimana, a Hutu moderate who had automatically become head of state following the president's death. Although Dallaire's UNAMIR force tried to protect Uwilingiyimana from the Hutu raid on her home, she was murdered by members of the Rwandan army.

Nor did the Hutu-targeted Belgian soldiers of UNAMIR escape the fate that had been planned for them. Ten Belgians were separated from the peacekeeping force and were tortured and killed, their bodies mutilated. As a result, all Belgian soldiers withdrew from Rwanda, as did most other foreign nationals, especially Americans and Europeans. Rwandans who worked for white foreigners, ranging from office assistants to family domestics, pleaded to be taken out of the country, to no avail.

Widespread Attacks

The Presidential Guards took command of the very early killing. Under direct orders from such hard-liners as Army Staff Director Colonel Théoneste Bagosora, they set up roadblocks to drag Tutsis from their cars and surrounded hospitals and churches in search of refuge seekers. The killings spread rapidly with the involvement of the Hutu militia known as the Interahamwe ("those who attack together"). The militias, which included the Hutu Youth, were all part of an organized Hutu Power movement that had long been training for the onslaught and that possessed hidden caches of weapons. The Hutu militia's killing frenzy quickly incited ordinary citizens, who were encouraged to use whatever weaponry was at hand, to attack their Tutsi neighbors. The identity cards that all Rwandans carried helped the Hutu attackers find their victims.

Having long given up their traditional religion, 65 percent of Rwandans were Catholic and about 15 percent were Protestant. Churches thus became places of refuge for the Tutsis. However, priests and pastors soon learned that they had no power to protect those who sought shelter. Some clergy were even complicit in the killings of Tutsi refugees, likely seeking their own immunity from the Hutu Power attackers.

At one church run by Polish missionaries, Dallaire's executive assistant Brent Beardsley "found 150 people, dead mostly, though some were still groaning, who had been attacked the night before. The Polish priests told us it had been incredibly well organized. The Rwandan army had cleared out the area, the gendarmerie had rounded up all the Tutsi, and the militia had hacked them to death."

School buildings were not immune to the violence. Children were among the choice victims of the Hutu killers, for the Hutu had vowed to prevent a future generation of Tutsi. Beardsley reported that at a school across the street from the church, "there were children, I don't know how many, forty, sixty, eighty children stacked up outside who had all been chopped up with machetes. Some of their mothers had heard them screaming and had come running, and the militia had killed them, too."

What happened to the piles of bodies of those who had been chopped to death by government soldiers, by the roaming militias, or by their very own neighbors? The rapidity of their accumulation made it impossible for morgues and cemeteries to accommodate them. Often, they lay as they fell. As a result, the population of stray dogs in Rwanda grew, until the Tutsi RPF took over the country in the late summer of 1994 and began shooting the scavenging animals.

International Awareness

The horror that was taking place in Rwanda was not a secret. Unlike in the case of the Cambodian genocide, Rwanda was not cut off from communication with the outside world. Paul Rusesabagina was in frequent contact by telephone with the directors of Sabena Airlines in Belgium. Josh Hammer, a *Newsweek* correspondent who briefly stayed at the Hôtel des Mille Collines in mid-April, reported seeing a gang of Interahamwe running in the street. "You could literally see the blood dripping off their clubs and machetes," he recalls.

Yet, aside from the small UNAMIR force of Lieutenant General Dallaire, the International Red Cross, and Médecins Sans Frontiéres (Doctors Without Borders), no foreign nation or other outside force intervened during the worst of the one hundred days of killing. In fact, on April 21, just as Dallaire was pleading for increases in UNAMIR forces and a free hand to use arms against the Hutu killers, the United Nations slashed the size of the force to only 270 troops. Dallaire managed through steady persuasion to keep 503.

By April 9 and 10, the US embassy in Kigali had been closed and more than 250 Americans had been evacuated. Rwandan embassy employees were refused sanctuary, and 35 were killed. As US Senate minority leader Bob Dole put it, "I don't think we have any national interest there. The Americans are out, and as far as I'm concerned, in Rwanda, that ought to be the end of it."

What had happened to the pledge that so many nations had made by ratifying the UN's 1948 Convention on the Prevention and Punishment of the Crime of Genocide (CPPCG)? After four decades of deliberation, the United States had finally, in 1988,

The Heroism of Paul Rusesabagina

The only largely successful stand against the butchery was that taken by a courageous Hutu, Paul Rusesabagina. As the manager of a large foreign-owned hotel in Rwanda, he found himself able to save more than 1,200 people through a combination of shrewdness and daring.

Rusesabagina had worked since 1984 at two Kigali luxury hotels owned by a Belgian airline. On April 9, two days after the slaughter in Kigali had begun, Rusesabagina was ordered to hand over the Hôtel des Diplomates, which he directed, to Colonel Bagosora, whose "interim government" planned to use it as a headquarters. Rusesabagina, his family, and a number of friends and neighbors soon found themselves held prisoner in the hotel. He staved off attempts to kill members of his entourage by handing out great sums of money. How long, though, could this tactic last?

Three days later, on April 12, Bagosora decided that the new headquarters was too accessible a target for the Tutsi raiders of the RPF and arranged for his company to flee Kigali for a more obscure command post. At the same time, Rusesabagina received a message from the Dutch manager of the hotel where he had worked until 1992— the Hôtel des Mille Collines. As a foreign national, the manager was preparing to leave the country. Could Rusesabagina take over for him?

After packing some thirty people into a hotel van, Rusesabagina followed the government convoy of armored vehicles as ordered. But as they approached the Hôtel des Mille Collines, he turned his vehicle onto the entry road. During the months that followed, the otherwise vacant international business-class hotel became a sanctuary for Hutu oppositionists and Tutsis, including orphaned children, women, and the elderly.

Paul Rusesabagina appears at a 2004 press conference for the film *Hotel Rwanda*, which depicts his heroism during the Rwandan genocide.

The hotel's $125-per-night rooms housed refugees of all ages and backgrounds, while Rusesabagina cajoled, pandered to, and bribed the army and Interahamwe units to spare his "guests" using cash from the hotel safe, liquor from its cellars, and Cuban cigars.

With the help of UNAMIR, Rusesabagina made a first attempt to evacuate the hotel's refugees on May 3, 1994, but Hutu roadblocks forced them to turn back. However, on May 27, the threat of the Tutsi RPF to execute Hutu government prisoners provided a bargaining chip that led to a first successful evacuation. The last of the 1,200 survivors left Rwanda on June 18.

joined with other nations in vowing to punish this crime against humanity. Of course, before any action could be taken, the crime had to be clearly defined as genocide. The question, however, of who decides a crime is genocide remained unanswered.

The administration of President Bill Clinton began to examine the killings in Rwanda. Were the perpetrators attacking an ethnic group? Yes. Was the purpose of the perpetrators to physically destroy the group in whole or in part? Yes. Were the perpetrators trying to wipe out the next generation of the ethnic group? Yes.

Yet the investigative spokesperson for the State Department was reluctant to use the word "genocide" with reference to Rwanda, lest the United States be forced to take military action to halt the killing. Only "acts of genocide" were being committed, according to the spokesperson's muddied conclusion. In private, though, senior officials were using the word "genocide" as soon as sixteen days after the start of the violence. Not until June 10, 1994, did Secretary of State Warren Christopher hesitantly state, "If there is any particular magic in calling it genocide, I have no hesitancy in saying that."

The Rwanda of July 1994 was a scene of widespread devastation. The nation's infrastructure had been heavily damaged. Water supplies had been disrupted, and electricity was scarce. Houses had been looted and vehicles destroyed. Untended crops had ripened and were rotting in the fields, where the refugee Tutsi—now moving back into the country—would graze their cattle.

France Intervenes

Would the United States have intervened if the Rwandan genocide had taken six months or a year instead of a mere hundred days? All that is known is that not a single top-level foreign policy meeting on the subject of military intervention was held in Washington during the entire three months of the slaughter.

Tutsi children at a refugee camp in Zaire surround a French soldier, one of many visiting the camp on June 24, 1994.

Meanwhile, Rwanda continued to be represented at the United Nations, at the time holding one of the rotating seats on the Security Council. As Samantha Power, author of *A Problem from Hell*, points out, "Neither the United States nor any other UN member state ever suggested that the representative of the genocidal government be expelled from the council."

Although individual members of Congress, the press, and other public media alluded frequently to the shameful indifference of the United States toward the horrors taking place in Rwanda, the Clinton administration remained firm in its conviction that intervention was not actually mandated under the CPPCG; the treaty only "enabled" intervention.

When a foreign military force did finally arrive in Rwanda, it came late in the conflict. It was France that stepped in. The European nation then led by President François Mitterand had long had a military and political interest in the regime of the slain Hutu president, Habyarimana. In fact, the private jet in which Habyarimana had lost his life had been a gift from the president of France.

Was Opération Turquoise, as the intervention was called, an effort to make amends for the pro-Hutu, anti-Tutsi stance of the French? If so, how effective was it? The intervention force arrived on June 23, 1994, only weeks before the RPF had taken sufficient control of Rwanda to be sworn in as its new government.

France's operation consisted of 2,500 heavily armed men in what was intended to be a largely humanitarian intervention. Although Opération Turquoise was purported to have a neutral purpose and to save as many Tutsi lives as possible, it was wildly cheered by the Interahamwe and actually put some of the RPF then approaching victory in danger.

On July 4, Kigali fell to Tutsi rebels; by July 14, the remnants of the Hutu interim government were fast disintegrating; and on July 19, the RPF took over as the official leader of a ravaged Rwanda. The French left soon after. At the same time, the tragic aftermath of the genocide began to unfold. Despite the promise that, this time, there would be a real power-sharing government, as many as 1.7 million Hutu refugees fled Rwanda, headed mainly for camps in neighboring Zaire and Tanzania.

The United States Steps In

At this point the United States came forward with some humanitarian aid for both the Hutu refugees in Zaire, dying of hunger and cholera, and for those Rwandans struggling to renew their lives inside the country.

However, in the eyes of many, these efforts seemed trivial compared with the assistance that could have been provided even without US military intervention. The United States could have backed UNAMIR, many argued; it could have influenced the United Nations to give Dallaire the troop strength he needed. The Clinton administration could have identified the crime as genocide earlier on and used its power to denounce the interim government of Rwanda and threaten its leaders with retribution.

Late in 1994, the UN Security Council set up a war crimes tribunal for Rwanda, but by that time it was too late for a single life to be saved. On March 25, 1998, President Clinton visited Rwanda and made an apology that was long overdue. "We in the United States and the world community did not do as much as we could have and should have done to try to limit what occurred … Never again must we be shy in the face of evidence."

Clinton's remorseful words seemed genuine. But how would they influence US and international actions in the face of future genocides? For, sadly, there would be more to come.

Chapter Six

MURDERING BOSNIA'S MUSLIMS

"**T**here is certainly life after such suffering, but there's never any joy," says Saliha Osmanovic, a mother whose entire family was killed in the violence surrounding the Bosnian War and the genocide against Bosnian Muslims. After her village was burned down, Osmanovic fled to a UN safe haven. Only later did she see video footage of her husband being captured. As he was being dragged away, he called up to their only surviving son. "I cannot describe the excruciating pain I experienced watching that," she says. The bodies of both father and son were found in mass graves. Osmanovic reburied them at the Potocari Memorial Centre in 2008.

Opposite: A man and his granddaughters are pictured at a United Nations refugee camp in 1995. All three were forced to flee their hometown in Bosnia during an ethnic cleansing against Muslims.

During the summer and fall of 1992, one hundred thousand people—80 percent of whom were Bosniak, or Bosnian Muslims—would be murdered outright or sent to detention camps to die. The Serb-run camps were as primitive as animal pens, lacking sanitary facilities or even space in which to move around. The majority of the women, who had all been sent off on their own, later reported that they had been sexually assaulted.

This assault on innocent town and city dwellers, whose families had lived for generations in the Yugoslav republic of Bosnia-Herzegovina, was a form of ethnic cleansing. Who were their Serb oppressors, and why did this attempt to drive them from their homeland take place after decades of multiethnic peace within the small, landlocked republic in the Balkan nation of Yugoslavia?

The Rise of Slobodan Milosevic

Josip Broz, popularly known as Tito, was Yugoslavia's leader for three and a half decades. His death in 1980 left the six autonomous republics that made up Yugoslavia without a single political figure capable of heading the nation. Nor did the Communist doctrine that Tito had successfully employed continue to have the power to unite the country as it had in the past.

After 1980, a rotating presidency was tried but proved unsuccessful. It appeared inevitable that the president of one of the six federated republics would eventually try to step into the leadership position formerly occupied by Tito. Such was the case. In 1991, Slobodan Milosevic, president of Serbia since 1989, made a move toward Serb nationalism—the extension of Serb power into all the other republics in which Serbs lived.

How could such a program be carried out in a nation where almost every republic had only a Serb minority—one that

"The Powder Keg of Europe"

Six countries—Albania, Bulgaria, Greece, parts of Romania and Turkey, and most of Yugoslavia—made up the Balkan Peninsula of southeastern Europe for most of the twentieth century. Early in the century, the region became known as "the powder keg of Europe" because so many wars sprang from the area, which was politically manipulated by the powerful kingdoms of the day.

The nation of Yugoslavia was a patchwork of ethnicities, languages, and religions. It consisted of Slavic peoples such as Serbs, Croats, and Slovenes, as well as Turks and Albanians. Serbs were Eastern Orthodox Christians and wrote their version of the Serbo-Croatian language in the Greek-derived Cyrillic alphabet, which is related to the Russian alphabet.

Croats and Slovenes were Roman Catholics and wrote Serbo-Croatian in the Latin alphabet. The descendants of the Turks who settled in Yugoslavia in the 1300s adopted Slavic culture to a degree but remained adherents of Islam, as did the Albanians living to the south.

The two world wars politically united the diverse peoples of Yugoslavia. World War II created a federal republic made up of six autonomous republics and two autonomous provinces. Serbia held sway over the others and contained the national capital, Belgrade.

However, the other independent republics—Bosnia, Croatia, Slovenia, Montenegro, and Macedonia—had their own capitals, presidents, and legislative bodies. Under the slogan "Brotherhood and Unity," wartime resistance leader and Communist strongman Josip Broz, or Tito, held the new Yugoslavia together from 1945 until his death in 1980. His death was followed by questions about which of the presidents of the six republics would take over and how the patchwork of Yugoslavia's peoples would fare now that the fabled and charismatic Tito was gone.

intermingled and even intermarried with non-Serbs? Croatia was inhabited principally by Roman Catholic Croats, although its border areas especially were comprised of more than 35 percent Eastern Orthodox Serbs. Bosnia was a mainly Muslim republic, but Croats and Serbs lived there, too.

Slovenia, in northwestern Yugoslavia, was a semi-alpine republic bordering Austria that was more culturally allied to western Europe. As the most prosperous of the six republics, Slovenia had long resented its mandated contributions to the economic development of the poorer republics, such as Muslim Macedonia, which was originally settled by Turks and then inhabited by Greeks and Bulgarians.

Nevertheless, for generations, people of many ethnic backgrounds and several different religions had enjoyed peaceful living conditions dwelling side by side in the region. Milosevic sought to disrupt this amity. He was prepared to "cleanse" the other republics of all but their Serb populations.

Wary of Serbia's encroaching nationalism, the republics of Slovenia, Croatia, and Bosnia made plans to secede, or disassociate, from the federated nation of Yugoslavia.

On June 25, 1991, Slovenia's president announced the independence of his republic, no longer to be affiliated with Yugoslavia. Then Milosevic dispatched the Yugoslav Peoples' Army to Slovenia. What followed was a minor war, lasting only ten days and resulting in forty-four military and a handful of civilian deaths. By July 8, Milosevic and Slovenia's president, Milan Kucan, had come to terms.

Milosevic had decided not to risk his larger aims for Slovenia, which counted almost no Serbs among its population. Threats of secession by other republics with large Serb populations would be met, however, with severe measures. Already, Croatia's president, Franjo Tudjman, had declared independence for his republic, also on June 25, 1991.

War Breaks Out

In August 1991, full-scale war broke out between Croatia and Serbia, and ethnic cleansing began in earnest. The effort to remove Croats from their own villages and give their holdings to their Serb neighbors was enforced not just by the Yugoslav Peoples' Army but also by Serb paramilitaries under the command of an army lieutenant colonel named Ratko Mladic. Brutal treatment of Croat civilians followed. They were robbed of their property, raped and beaten, and confined to overcrowded prison cells.

November 1991 saw the fall of the town of Vukovar, on Croatia's eastern border with Serbia. Although Vukovar's population was just 37.4 percent Serb, the Serbs claimed it for their own. After the three-month siege, "Corpses of people and animals littered the streets. Grisly skeletons of buildings still burned, barely a square inch had escaped damage. Serbian volunteers, wild-eyed, roared down the streets, their pockets full of looted treasures." Still, by the end of 1991, an embattled Croatia had won its independence. However, it had lost nearly half its territory to Serbia, and much of it was occupied by the enemy.

Bosnia-Herzegovina, most often referred to as Bosnia, was the next republic to attempt secession. Bosnia's declaration of independence in March 1992 was recognized by both the United States and the European community. Alija Izetbegovic, a Muslim, had been president of Bosnia since 1990. He represented not only Bosnia's largest ethnic group—its 44-percent Muslim population—but also its smaller percentages of Serbs (32 percent) and Croats (19 percent).

A new Bosnian Serb leader, Radovan Karadzic, took charge of the political and military assault on Bosnia. Among the first strikes was a major attack on the capital of Sarajevo, a city dominated by mosques and minarets, but one in which Muslims, Serbs, and

Croats had lived together for five hundred years. Set among steep hills, Sarajevo had also been the site of the 1984 Winter Olympics.

The Siege of Sarajevo

On April 5, 1992, as thousands of unarmed Sarajevo citizens marched through the city protesting ethnic strife and proclaiming tolerance, the first shots from Serb artillery rang out. This was the beginning of the siege of Sarajevo, which would last nearly four years.

During that time, Sarajevo would become crowded with refugees from the surrounding towns and villages that had been overtaken by the Serbs. The Bosnian Serbs blockaded the roads and shut down the airport, preventing the besieged city from receiving food, water, medicine, and other vital supplies, and frequently shelling its four hundred thousand residents. Sniper attacks were common.

Air assaults, too, took place at the hands of a now-well-organized Serb military force of eighty thousand under the command of Major General (soon to be Lieutenant General) Mladic, working alongside political leader Karadzic. Cease-fires brokered by western nations were constantly violated. European powers and the United States provided only humanitarian aid in the form of airdrops and relief convoys, the latter arranged by the United Nations with the grudging permission of the Bosnian Serbs.

Not until August 1995, when the western powers of the North Atlantic Treaty Organization (NATO) finally voted to bomb the Bosnian Serb positions around Sarajevo, did the Serbs begin to loosen their grip on the battered city. By the time the siege ended, twelve thousand civilians had been killed in Sarajevo and more than fifty thousand had been wounded.

A woman is pictured in Sarajevo during the four-year siege of the city, during which thousands died.

During that period, the Serbs vigorously pursued their policy of ethnic cleansing in Bosnia's other towns and villages. On August 14, 1992, US diplomat Richard Holbrooke witnessed a scene in the small city of Banja Luka in northern Bosnia, where "at close to gunpoint, Muslims are signing papers giving up their personal property, either to neighbors or in exchange for the right to leave Bosnia. Then they are herded onto buses headed for the border … Some leave quietly, others crying. This is the end of their lives in an area their families have lived in for centuries."

Many of the Muslim refugees never reached the border. Their lives ended in detention camps reminiscent of the Nazi death camps of World War II. As reported by journalist Roy Gutman of the New York newspaper *Newsday*, "Heads bowed and hands clasped behind their backs, the Muslim prisoners lined up before their Serb captors. One by one they sat on the metal stool and then knelt to have their heads shaved." Those who did not die of starvation and disease in the Serb camps became victims of either random or selective killings, preceded by orders to dig their own graves.

Death Camps and International Intervention

The massacres in Bosnia were known to the outside world as early as May 1992. From within Bosnia came reports by eyewitnesses who had been present at the earliest ethnic cleansing procedures. The reports reached UN Secretary General Boutros Boutros-Ghali directly through Bosnia's ambassador to the United Nations. Journalists, aid workers, and even travelers came upon scenes in Bosnia of people being forcibly ejected from their homes, rounded up, beaten, jeered at, and threatened, then evacuated in buses or cattle cars. By the end of 1992, "almost two million Bosnians—nearly half the population—had lost their homes."

By August 1992, crowding and starvation in the death camps of Bosnia had reached such an intense degree that a writer for the *Guardian*, a British newspaper, attested to the following: "The men are at various stages of human decay and affliction; the bones of their elbows and wrists protrude like pieces of jagged stone from the pencil thin stalks to which their arms have been reduced." Television reports transmitted scenes of horror to the outside world.

Although the United Nations, the European community, and the United States knew about the atrocities being committed in Bosnia, no action other than weak UN peacekeeper support was taken. The UN Security Council refused to lift the arms embargo placed on Bosnia at the start of the conflict, even though its antagonist, Serbia, had boldly violated the order.

In a January 1993 memorandum from US diplomat Richard Holbrooke to the incoming administration of President Bill Clinton, the following observations and recommendations were made. Holbrooke, who had witnessed the scene in Bosnia during the past year, urged that the UN embargo be lifted at the behest of the United States.

Holbrooke also suggested that the United States brand such Bosnian Serb leaders as Karadzic and Mladic war criminals, to be harshly dealt with by the international community after the conflict ended. He further advised that in order "to save as many lives as possible in Bosnia" the United States and other nations should create "some sort of ad hoc military coalition."

Holbrooke did not feel that the international community should get involved in a ground war in the region. He did, however, favor "Direct use of force against the Serbs: Bombing the Bosnian Serbs and even Serbia proper if necessary." Holbrooke's memorandum received no reply from Washington, nor did other nations respond to his suggestion. The genocide in Bosnia would continue.

The Srebrenica Massacres

East of Sarajevo, close to the border with Serbia, lies the city of Srebrenica, named for the silver mining that once took place in the vicinity. The city's population of thirty-seven thousand was 75 percent Muslim and 25 percent Serb. Early in the conflict between Serbia and Bosnia, it had been defended with some success.

In April 1993, however, as Serb advances against this part of Bosnia became more intense, the United Nations took action, declaring Srebrenica and five other towns and cities in the region to be "safe areas." A UN Protection Force (UNPROFOR) would police the "safe areas" to oversee a hoped-for cessation of fighting in the battle between the Bosnian defenders and the increasingly threatening Bosnian Serbs, as well as to facilitate the entry of humanitarian aid and relief supplies to the besieged cities.

Lightly armed and backed with no more authority than the blue flag of the United Nations, the 7,400 troops contributed by member nations were hardly in a position to maintain disarmament. The Bosnian Serbs had already knocked out the water supplies, electricity, and other basic services in the region.

The UNPROFOR assignment limped along for two years until, on July 6, 1995, General Mladic unleashed his frustrations on the "safe area" of Srebrenica. In a week that began with shelling, the Bosnian Serbs carried out, in the words of Richard Holbrooke, "the biggest single mass murder in Europe since World War II."

Upon entering the city, Mladic's forces rounded up men and boys by the thousands, shooting them on the spot, herding them into the soccer stadium to be executed, or shoving them onto buses to be taken to adjacent killing sites. The Dutch UNPROFOR peacekeepers, of which there were 370, were taken hostage. In all, some eight thousand Muslim men and boys were murdered in the fall of Srebrenica. Untold numbers of women and girls were raped.

Hungry Bosnian prisoners of war are shown in an overcrowded detainment cell at the Manjaca concentration camp, where an estimated fifteen thousand Croats and Bosnians were imprisoned.

Pleas from the Dutch commander at Srebrenica for air strikes against the Serbs were denied as being too "dangerous," despite past humiliations of UNPROFOR troops. At other safe areas the Serbs had "handcuffed [French soldiers] to trees and telephone poles. The world's press was invited to film these men standing miserably in the broiling sun … waving white flags of surrender, to the horror of the new French President, Jacques Chirac."

NATO Steps In

When would the American, French, British, and other members of NATO finally take action against the slaughter that had made the United Nations' efforts at controlling it a mockery? Since taking office in 1993, President Clinton had remained indecisive regarding involvement in Bosnia, fearful of being drawn into a stalemate or, as the Bosnian Serb leader Radovan Karadzic threateningly termed it, "another Vietnam." Srebrenica, however, with its ruthless civilian killings and its massive death pits, left little choice for Clinton but to intervene.

On August 30, 1995, a coordinated NATO bombing by more than sixty aircraft pounded Bosnian Serb positions around the still-besieged city of Sarajevo. The massive air strikes of Operation Deliberate Force continued into September of 1995 and took out strategic Serb emplacements in and around the other safe areas that had been under siege.

The NATO bombings finally crippled the efforts of Milosevic and his chief henchmen to continue the genocide of Bosnian Muslims. But it was too late for the one hundred thousand victims of the Serbs' ethnic cleansing campaign, who now lay nameless— most of them intentionally stripped of their identities before execution—in mass graves.

Peace Negotiations

At last, a draft for a peace agreement was reached, with Holbrooke as chief negotiator between the western powers and the presidents of the three former Yugoslav republics—Milosevic of Serbia, Alija Izetbegovic of Bosnia, and Franjo Tudjman of Croatia. They met for talks in Dayton, Ohio. The presidents of Bosnia and Croatia were understandably hostile toward and distrustful of Milosevic. The punishment of war criminals and the future ethnic composition of Bosnia were of special concern. Nearly two million Bosnian Muslims had been displaced. Where in Bosnia would they relocate, and should a portion of Bosnia be assigned to its onetime Bosnian Serb population?

In what has come to be seen by many analysts as an unsatisfactory and even perilous solution, the territory formerly known as Bosnia was divided into two approximately equal-sized entities. The newly named Bosnian Federation was to consist of a majority of Bosnian Muslims (53 percent) and a smaller number (41 percent) of Bosnian Croats. The other half of the former Bosnia was to be known as Republika Srpska and would be occupied by Bosnian Serbs, who would make up nearly 90 percent of its population.

Nonetheless, the Dayton Agreement was signed in Paris on December 14, 1995, by the Americans as well as the leaders of France, the United Kingdom, Germany, and Russia. To monitor and implement its terms, militarily if necessary, a NATO-led Implementation Force (IFOR) was deployed. IFOR proved more effective in maintaining and enforcing peace than had UNPROFOR.

However, according to Holbrooke, "the arrest of Karadzic and Mladic was the most critical issue that was not resolved at

Dayton. I repeated … that if the two men, particularly Karadzic, the founder and leader of a still-unrepentant separatist movement, remained at large, full implementation of the agreement would be impossible." They would not be held to task for the crimes they had committed for more than a decade.

Genocide in Kosovo

Having succeeded in obtaining 49 percent of Bosnia for its Serb population, Milosevic left Dayton a respected negotiator and returned to Belgrade. However, his ambition to expand his domain into a Greater Serbia had not died with the losses in Croatia and Bosnia. As early as 1987, Milosevic had seized on the idea of expanding Serbia by driving out the 90 percent Albanian population of the autonomous province of Kosovo in southern Yugoslavia, which shared part of its border with Albania.

Six hundred years earlier, in 1389, the Serbs had suffered a massive defeat by the Turks on the battlefield known as Kosovo Polje, and the area had subsequently become the home of Muslim peoples, especially Albanians. In 1989, when he became president of Serbia, Milosevic began to suppress the rights of the Muslim majority and to destroy the autonomy of the province, favoring its small Serb minority. Kosovo, in turn, began a movement for secession and independence.

In 1998, three years after Dayton, Milosevic was carrying out a campaign of ethnic cleansing and outright murder against Kosovar Albanians. Hundreds of thousands of people became refugees as the Kosovo Liberation Army (KLA) fought the Serbian military and police.

Ultimatums from NATO to Milosevic to halt the genocide in Kosovo had no effect and, from March to June 1999, western

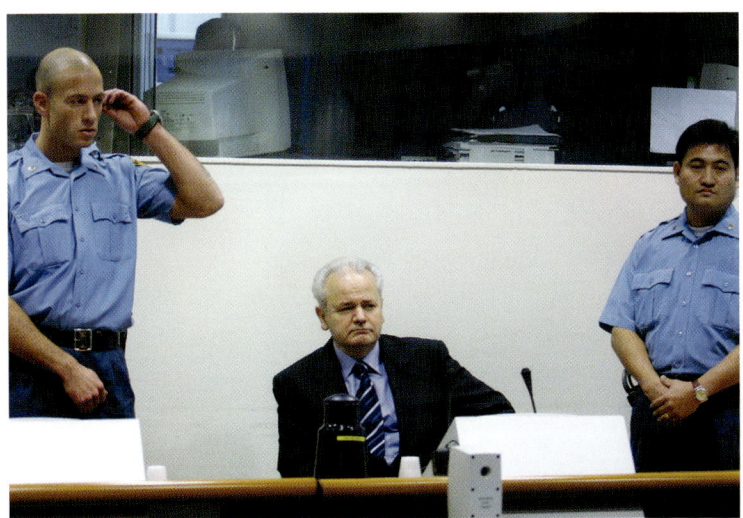

Slobodan Milosevic (*center*), former president of Serbia, is pictured during a pretrial hearing for a war crimes tribunal in The Hague in 2002.

powers carried out their threat of air strikes against targets in Kosovo and Serbia. Operation Allied Force knocked out major public services and vital commercial installations in the Serbian capital of Belgrade. There appeared to be no other way of curbing the feverish nationalist onslaughts of the Serbian president.

After Milosevic's forced withdrawal from Kosovo, one hundred thousand Serb inhabitants (nearly half the Kosovo Serb population) were forced to flee. As public opinion turned against Milosevic, his grip on the presidency began to loosen. A new coalition of leaders pledging themselves to multiethnic peace rose to power and, following the disputed elections of 2000, Milosevic was forced to resign the presidency under accusations of wrongdoing and amid demonstrations calling for his punishment. On March 31, 2001, his own government arrested him on suspicion of corruption, abuse of power, and embezzlement.

Seeking Justice

In 2002, charges of crimes against humanity, violations of wartime behavior, breaches of the Geneva Conventions, and genocide in Croatia, Bosnia, and Kosovo were awaiting Milosevic at the International Criminal Tribunal for the Former Yugoslavia (ICTY) in The Hague in the Netherlands.

Obstinate to the last, the man who had fomented genocidal war in Europe insisted on conducting his own defense. His trial was still in progress after nearly five years when he died in his prison cell on March 11, 2006, apparently of a heart attack. Humanity was thus robbed of seeing justice carried out against the brutal leader.

The ICTY had been founded in 1993 for the specific purpose of dealing with the war crimes and crimes against humanity that had taken place in the former Yugoslavia since 1991. The court's first conviction for genocide was that of Radislav Krstic, the general who was second-in-command to Mladic and who had ordered the massacre of eight thousand men and boys in Srebrenica in July 1995. In August 2001, the fifty-three-year-old Krstic was sentenced to forty-six years in prison.

Relatives of Srebrenica victims were dissatisfied with the sentence (the tribunal's maximum sentence is life imprisonment). "Let him go and come back to us," a Srebrenica woman exclaimed. "We will give him a verdict. For 10,000 of our sons, only 46 years! His people have ripped my son from my arms." The families of the victims were further incensed when, in 2004, Krstic's sentence was reduced on appeal to thirty-five years, on the grounds that he was not a principal perpetrator of the genocide. The court concluded that he was only aiding and abetting, as ordered by his superior officers.

As late as 2008, the indicted Mladic, who had disappeared in 2001, and Karadzic, who had vanished in 1996, had not been apprehended. But in July 2008, Karadzic, one of the world's most wanted war criminals, was arrested. The fugitive had radically disguised his appearance and had been living openly in Belgrade as a practitioner of alternative medicine. In 2016, Karadzic was sentenced to forty years in prison.

Mladic, who had been nicknamed the "butcher of Bosnia," was arrested in Serbia in 2011 and sentenced to life in prison for genocide, war crimes, and crimes against humanity in 2017. Relatives of many of the victims had flown in to see the verdict. Afterwards, Fikret Alic stood before a crowd of journalists, holding up a copy of *TIME* magazine from 1992. On the cover was a photo of Alic, emaciated in a prison camp. "Justice has won and the war criminal has been convicted," he said.

To date, eighty-three people have been convicted in the Yugoslav war crimes trials.

Chapter Seven

MASSACRING THE ROHINGYA

As hundreds of thousands of people began to flood across the border from Myanmar to Bangladesh in August of 2017, the stories they carried with them were appalling. The refugees were Muslims, part of an ethnic minority called the Rohingya that had been brutally persecuted for decades in the Buddhist-majority country of Myanmar. Now, the Myanmar military was carrying out widespread attacks on Rohingya villages.

In the first month, at least 6,700 Rohingya were killed—among them, upwards of 730 children. Many more would be murdered, tortured, or brutally assaulted as, over the next several months, between 687,000 and 725,000 people arrived in refugee camps

Opposite: Rohingya refugees line up near the Bangladesh–Myanmar border as they try to flee violence in Myanmar in 2017.

in Bangladesh—more than two-thirds of the entire Rohingya population of Myanmar as of early 2017. The Myanmar military partially or completely destroyed an estimated 392 Rohingya villages, often by burning them to the ground.

In 2018, a United Nations fact-finding mission published a report that called for Myanmar's military generals to be charged with genocide before an international court. "I have never been confronted by crimes as horrendous and on such a scale as these," said Marzuki Darusman, chair of the group. Yet these crimes were only the latest in a long history of discrimination and violence against the Rohingya people.

Who Are the Rohingya?

More than one million Rohingya lived in the Southeast Asian country of Myanmar—also known as Burma—before the attacks of 2017. Of these, eight in ten lived in the Rakhine state, in the northwest region of the country.

The Rohingya are an ethnic minority group comprised primarily of people of the Muslim faith. They speak a language called Rohingya or Ruaingga, distinct from what is spoken elsewhere in Myanmar. Many Rohingya insist their roots in Myanmar can be traced back as far as the ninth century to Muslim traders in the area.

The Rohingya pass down their history through *taranas*, a combination of songs and drawings. These stories not only recall the many generations who have lived in the Rakhine state, but also communicate a sense of identity. What's more, they recall a long history of persecution, displacement, and resistance. Many Rohingya have used drawings or songs to explain to their children why they are living in exile.

For its part, the government of Myanmar insists that the Rohingya arrived in the country much more recently, during

Twelve-year-old Rohingya refugee Kurshida shows her drawing of an attack on her village, during which the military set fire to her home.

British rule of the region between 1824 and 1948. During this time, many laborers from India and what is today called Bangladesh migrated to Myanmar to work, and the government argues that the Rohingya were among them. Because of this, when Myanmar achieved independence from the British in 1948, many Rohingya were not included in the Union Citizenship Act. The government saw their presence in the country as "illegal." Since 1982, all Rohingya have been denied citizenship, and even though Myanmar has 135 official ethnic groups, the Rohingya are not among them. In fact, the government even denies that "Rohingya" is a legitimate term, often insisting on calling them Bengali, which implies they are from India or Bangladesh. Bangladesh, meanwhile, has denied that the Rohingya are Bangladeshi.

Other countries in the region, including Thailand and Malaysia, have refused to take in many Rohingya who have left Myanmar seeking safety, better living conditions, and a new life. In a period of just three months in 2015, twenty-five thousand migrants from Bangladesh—an estimated 40–60 percent of whom were Rohingya—attempted to travel by sea to Malaysia, Indonesia, or Thailand with the help of smugglers. Three hundred died during these journeys.

Many were trying to flee a system of institutionalized discrimination against the Rohingya and Muslims living in Myanmar. Because they have been denied citizenship, the Rohingya find it more difficult to access all kinds of basic services, including health care and education. They have been limited in their ability to find jobs, travel, practice their religion, and even marry.

The Violence Worsens

In 2012, as many as 140,000 Rohingya were forced to flee after a spate of violence perpetrated by some extremist and nationalist Buddhist groups. After these attacks, Sittwe, once a multicultural city on the Bay of Bengal, was mostly emptied of Muslims. Five years later, many of the people living there told Hannah Beech, a *New York Times* reporter, that no Muslims had ever sold their wares in the Sittwe bazaar—despite the fact that Beech herself had seen them in plenty just a few years before.

These denials seemed to fall in step with a broader campaign by Myanmar security forces that, according to a 2017 report from the United Nations, had essentially attempted to erase all traces of the Rohingya from Myanmar. According to Rohingya lawyer U Kyaw Hla Aung, it is part of a decades-long effort to deny the Rohingya's identity. "We are people with our own history and traditions," he told Beech. "How can they pretend we are nothing?" Kyaw Hla Aung was speaking with Beech over the phone in December 2017 from an internment camp inside Myanmar, where he said his family was going hungry because government officials weren't distributing all the food that had been provided through international aid.

Kyaw Hla Aung was not alone. Following the violence of 2012, many Rohingya were confined to camps in rural areas of Rakhine without access to health care or education. They weren't allowed to leave these internment camps without authorization. In 2013, international nongovernmental organization Human Rights Watch declared that the government of Myanmar was conducting a campaign of ethnic cleansing.

Since 2012, violence in Rakhine state has escalated. The year 2016 saw a series of clashes that left many, including children and infants, dead or injured and tens of thousands displaced. However, the international community at times struggled to determine who was fighting whom, since human-rights monitors and journalists were prohibited from entering the area.

In 2015, a legal analysis conducted at Yale Law School's Allard K. Lowenstein International Human Rights Clinic found "strong evidence of genocide against the Rohingya population." In November 2016, Adama Dieng, special adviser on the prevention of genocide for the United Nations, called for an investigation into allegations of targeted attacks against the Rohingya. But the crisis that would draw the world's attention was yet to come.

Thousands Massacred

On August 25, 2017, militants from the Arakan Rohingya Salvation Army (ARSA) attacked more than thirty police posts in Myanmar. Twelve security forces members and at least fifty-nine insurgents were killed.

Retaliation by the Myanmar government was swift and deadly. An estimated 6,700 Rohingya—and by some accounts, thousands more—would die in the month of violence that ensued. During this time, nearly four hundred villages were destroyed, and sexual assault against women and girls was widespread and brutal.

The government called these attacks "clearance operations" against ARSA members, but the international community agreed that their real target was in fact much broader: they were attacking anyone from the Rohingya ethnic group, which was predominantly Muslim. The attacks, then, were motivated by both ethnic and religious intolerance.

As the international community decried the massacres, the Myanmar government insisted that the Rohingya had burned their own homes, a claim that drew widespread skepticism. Meanwhile, the government declared ARSA a terrorist group.

Living as Refugees

The first refugees started flooding over the border into Bangladesh on August 25. In the ensuing months, as many as 725,000 would be displaced.

A year after the attacks, the *Guardian* newspaper reported that as many as one million refugees were still living in or near the city of Cox's Bazar in Bangladesh, which was among the largest refugee camps in the world and which some organizations had begun referring to as Bangladesh's fourth-largest city. They were living in an area that was only about 5 square miles (13 sq km).

Makeshift shelters covered with tarps, constructed on the side of sandy hills, faced the threat of landslides or collapse at the height of monsoon season in August 2018. However, in the last year, the Rohingya with help from international aid organizations had begun to make improvements: they had built wells for water, drainage ditches, and pit latrines.

According to estimates by the United Nations International Children's Emergency Fund, more than half of the refugees living in these camps were children. Jason Beaubien, an NPR journalist who visited in August 2018, witnessed a group of about two dozen boys playing with toy airplanes they had made out of

Aung San Suu Kyi: "The World Is Waiting"

Myanmar is home to Aung San Suu Kyi, who won a Nobel Peace Prize in 1991 for standing up to the country's oppressive military regime. The Nobel Committee at that time called her "an outstanding example of the power of the powerless."

Suu Kyi was under house arrest for fifteen years because of her resistance to Myanmar's ruling generals, but in 2016, she rose to political power after a democratic election. She was not permitted to become president but took on the title of "state counsellor" and became the country's de facto leader, a role she still held as of late 2018.

Yet for all her work to stand up for the powerless, Suu Kyi has repeatedly refused to admit that any human-rights abuses were being inflicted upon the Rohingya people. Even as refugee camps overflowed with hundreds of thousands of Rohingya in 2017, Suu Kyi called them "terrorists" and insisted that a "huge iceberg of misinformation" had spread throughout the international community.

Many denounced Suu Kyi's refusal to defend the Rohingya, and some even called for her Nobel Prize to be revoked. Canada revoked Suu Kyi's honorary citizenship in October 2018 because of her continued inaction.

"Over the last several years, I have repeatedly condemned this tragic and shameful treatment. I am still waiting for my fellow Nobel Laureate Aung San Suu Kyi to do the same," wrote Malala Yousafzai, who in 2014 became the youngest Nobel laureate in history. "The world is waiting and the Rohingya Muslims are waiting."

Those in the international community who still support Suu Kyi insist that she must be pragmatic in a political environment in which the military still maintains control over one in four parliamentary seats and several government ministries.

soda bottles, bamboo, and scraps of metal. This was how many children in these camps spent their days, since they didn't have adequate access to education.

Meanwhile, adult refugees weren't legally permitted to work in Bangladesh, so they had to get by on bimonthly rations of lentils, cooking oil, and rice provided by the UN World Food Program. Even so, many had set up small businesses within the camps—tea shops, market stalls, even a barbershop. What their future would hold, and whether they could ever return to their homes, remained unclear.

In November 2017, a repatriation deal was signed between Myanmar and Bangladesh that would allow 650,000 Rohingya refugees to return to Myanmar voluntarily over a period of two years. However, some in the international community expressed skepticism over the terms of the deal, and many Rohingya were fearful at the prospect of returning to a country where they didn't feel protected.

"We have been tortured, killed and our houses burnt, we want Myanmar citizenship and ID cards saying we are Rohingya. I don't want to go to another camp in Myanmar," refugee Syed Alam told the Al Jazeera news agency.

Human Rights Watch, meanwhile, called for these returns to be independently monitored to ensure that Rohingya property was restored and refugees received fair treatment.

In the months after the attacks, many in Myanmar remained doubtful that any kind of peaceful resolution could be reached. "The Rohingya are finished in our country," said U Kyaw Min, a Rohingya politician and president of the Democracy and Human Rights Party in Myanmar. "Soon we will all be dead or gone."

International Response

Both governmental and nongovernmental organizations—including the UN and Amnesty International—have denounced the treatment of the Rohingya, calling them "the most persecuted minority in the world."

The administration of US president Donald Trump declared in November 2017 that the events of a few months earlier had constituted ethnic cleansing, which is a crime against humanity. It also announced that the US government would pursue limited sanctions against some of the military leaders involved.

In March 2018, the UN resolved to task an independent fact-finding mission with the investigation of these alleged crimes. On August 27, 2018, the mission submitted a report that confirmed massacres, mass sexual assault, burning, and looting in fifty-four locations throughout Rakhine. According to the report, at least ten thousand Rohingya had been killed. In October, Darusman, chair of the fact-finding mission, called on the UN Security Council to refer the matter to the International Criminal Court, which prosecutes crimes against humanity on the international stage. The ICC had already launched a preliminary investigation into the events surrounding August 2017.

Darusman also recommended sanctions against specific Myanmar officials and an arms embargo that would limit the entry of weapons into the country. As of late 2018, however, it remained unclear what the international community could or would do to help these displaced people.

Chapter Eight

INTERVENTION AND JUSTICE

In cases where the deliberate and systematic destruction of a people for reasons of race, ethnicity, nationality, or religion has taken place, and intervention is absent or inadequate, can justice ever be served? The question of whether military intervention is morally necessary or illegal—and whether it's even effective—yields no easy answers. The international community has also tried nonmilitary means of intervention. Which methods are most effective remains a matter of debate.

Reasons for Inaction

In the face of all the genocides the world has experienced, why have so few military interventions

Opposite: Rohingya refugees, pictured here in May 2015, receive food donated by the Acehnese people of Indonesia.

taken place? Understanding the context of each conflict is necessary before we can comprehend this inaction.

One of the reasons often cited by American officialdom for the failure to take action during the Rwandan genocide was the involvement of the United States, between 1992 and 1994, in the northeastern African country of Somalia. In 1992, during the administration of President George H. W. Bush, the US Army had undertaken a humanitarian mission in the desert-like nation that borders the Indian Ocean. The operation, though, had gone horribly wrong. Was the failed American military intervention in Somalia a justifiable excuse for denying adequate troop strength to UNAMIR in Rwanda?

The failure to directly help the six million Jews of Europe who died under the Nazi regime may indeed have been caused by disbelief, the inability to accept that evil of such magnitude could exist. Recall the response of Supreme Court justice Felix Frankfurter when Polish emissary Jan Karski presented him with proof of the existence of the death camps. Frankfurter, himself a Jew, seemed unable to believe Karski's claims.

Other reasons for inaction in the face of genocide abound. Officials voice the argument that emotional factors are too likely to draw the nation into dangerous situations; that US intervention may only increase the bloodshed; and that it is sometimes difficult to be sure the conflict at hand can be defined as genocide. In an article for the *Oxford Research Encyclopedia of International Studies*, Taylor B. Seybolt points out that, during the Cold War era (1945–1990), military intervention for humanitarian reasons "contained the danger of escalation to a catastrophic international war with the Soviet Union and the Eastern bloc." After the Cold War, there have been more such interventions, though not necessarily in cases of genocide.

Military Intervention

Is military action, such as the NATO bombing of the Bosnian Serb army emplacements above Sarajevo in 1995, always necessary? Is it effective? Would an earlier response to Sarajevo and Kosovo have saved lives and made for less violence and destruction in the long run?

Seybolt writes that there has been surprisingly little analysis of just how effective military intervention is in the case of humanitarian crises. Instead, analysts are divided into two camps: those who focus on the legality and practicality of intervention, and those who emphasize the moral necessity of it. Many have sought ways to make such interventions more effective, but whether they are in the first place remains unclear.

Proponents of military intervention point to the success of the NATO-led intervention in Kosovo and insist that, because all humans have inalienable, basic rights, the international community has a responsibility to step in when those rights are being violated. Many advocate for multilateral intervention— that is, intervention in which multiple countries collaborate to stop a genocide.

Opponents say that military intervention is against international law, does not respect state sovereignty, and is ineffective. They warn that it is similar to colonialism: "it is an instrument of strong states' domination over weak ones." They also point out that violence within a state is sometimes a necessary step in establishing political order. As Seybolt explains it, "The principle of nonintervention reduces the risk of war, respects the differences between societies, and allows for the development of rights within societies rather than imposing them from outside."

One rare example of a swift military response to genocide took place in August 2014, when terrorist group the Islamic

A woman holds a sign at a demonstration in support of the Yazidi people in the Netherlands in 2014.

State of Iraq and Syria (ISIS) killed or kidnapped an estimated 9,900 Yazidi people, while hundreds of thousands of people fled their homes. The Yazidis are a minority group of around seven hundred thousand people living in northern Iraq. They are primarily ethnically Kurdish and adhere to an ancient religion derived from Zoroastrianism, Christianity, and Islam. In the eighteenth and nineteenth centuries alone, they were the victims of seventy-two genocidal massacres.

In August 2014, forty thousand Yazidis found themselves trapped as ISIS forces closed in on their region. Within a few days, US president Barack Obama authorized airstrikes against ISIS, calling the attacks on Yazidis "genocide." These airstrikes, however, were limited. Obama was in the process of withdrawing

American troops from Iraq after a war there that had raged for more than a decade. "I will not allow the United States to be dragged into another war in Iraq," Obama said. Aircraft were also sent to drop food and water for the besieged people, and the United States reportedly provided weapons and ammunition to Iraqi military forces and Kurdish fighters opposing ISIS. The United Nations, meanwhile, created a corridor through which people could flee. More airstrikes by an international coalition were launched in September.

Thousands of refugees escaped, and there is some evidence that the airstrikes, in tandem with other efforts, may have helped to slow the advance of ISIS in the region. However, ISIS's persecution of the Yazidis because of their religion would go on for several more years. Those who had been kidnapped were subjected to enslavement, horrific sexual abuse, and torture. Some children were forced to work as soldiers. ISIS forcibly mutilated some women so that they would be unable to have children.

ISIS reached its peak territory in October 2014. Afterwards, the Iraqi army with the help of Kurd forces and some support from the international community slowly began to reclaim territory. In 2017, women were still being freed from ISIS, returning to their families shocked and traumatized. Many Yazidis, meanwhile, were still living in refugee camps. It remains unclear whether more airstrikes might have helped, but some military intervention did seem to aid those Yazidi refugees who fled the fighting—and may have saved some of their lives.

Nonmilitary Intervention

The United States and other members of the international community also have nonmilitary methods for stopping genocide at their disposal. Perpetrators can be expelled from the United Nations, their embassies abroad can be closed, foreign assets can

The UN Convention on Genocide and the United States

Genocide was identified and defined by the UN Convention on the Prevention and Punishment of the Crime of Genocide (CPPCG) in 1948. The United States, however, did not ratify the treaty until 1988.

Although President Harry Truman had called for ratification in June 1949, both Congress and Truman's successors looked at the international treaty as a source of possible threats against the United States. Was the United States entirely free of genocidal guilt? There were so many ethnic, racial, religious, and cultural groups, past and present, who might bring charges. Potential accusations ranged from the persecution and mass killing of Native Americans to contemporary assaults on homosexuals, African Americans, Jews, and immigrants.

Almost single-handedly, Senator William Proxmire of Wisconsin took up the cause of the ratification of the CPPCG. For nineteen years, from 1967 to 1986, he gave almost daily speeches before Congress—3,211 in all—urging acceptance of the treaty. But it was a tactical blunder on the part of President Ronald Reagan in 1985 that finally aroused strong enough support for the CPPGG that Congress could no longer hold out.

To commemorate the fortieth anniversary of the end of World War II, President Reagan traveled to Germany in May 1985 to lay a wreath on a cemetery for German military war dead. No arrangement had been made, however, for him to visit a Holocaust site in remembrance of the war's Jewish victims. Popular outrage ensued.

Congress ratified the treaty on genocide in 1986. On signing it into law in 1988, President Reagan declared, "We finally close the circle today. I am delighted to fulfill the promise made by Harry Truman to all the peoples of the world and especially to the Jewish people."

be frozen, and economic sanctions can be applied. Genocidal authorities can be threatened with prosecution in international courts. Well-armed peacekeeping forces can be provided through the United Nations. At the same time, refugees from genocide can be housed in safe shelters that are capable of sustaining health and life.

Nonmilitary humanitarian intervention on the part of both governmental and nongovernmental agencies has also brought relief to victims of genocide over and over again.

Citizens and companies have a role to play, too, argues Aliza Luft, an associate professor of sociology at the University of California, Los Angeles, in a 2018 article for the *Washington Post*. She points to the efforts of the Enough Project, which has encouraged major tech companies to offer conflict-free products. These efforts, along with the work of civilian activists, have aimed to defund warlord-backed mining companies in the Democratic Republic of the Congo, which has suffered six million civilian deaths and mass rape since 1996.

Likewise, as genocide against Muslims rages on in the country of Myanmar, the Myanmar Foreign Investment Tracking Project has demanded that more than one hundred companies explain their investments in Myanmar and affirm their commitment to human rights. Companies that seem to be supporting the murderous Myanmar regime should be boycotted and targeted by social-media campaigns for their complicity in the genocide, Luft writes. The International Campaign for Rohingya is doing just that through its #NoBusinessWithGenocide efforts.

Genocide Tribunals

The international community has sought to establish tribunals to bring perpetrators of genocide to justice after the fact, but many of these have been, for the victims, too little, too late. Other efforts, such as the International Criminal Court's indictment of Sudanese president Omar al-Bashir, lack sufficient authority to carry out what they've started. Nearly a decade after he was first indicted, al-Bashir remains the president of Sudan and hasn't answered for his actions.

Here are a few examples of such tribunals and what they have achieved in the last century.

The Nuremberg Trials

At the end of World War II, Adolf Hitler committed suicide. There was no way, then, to make him answer for his crimes in a court of law. However, the international community did want to bring his associates to justice. Their efforts culminated in the Nuremberg Trials, which took place in 1945 and 1946.

No permanent international court of criminal justice existed at the time, so the trials were held at the behest of the United States, Great Britain, France, and the Soviet Union. At the first Nuremberg Trial, the prosecuting nations indicted twenty-four and tried twenty-one of Nazi Germany's major war criminals. Among them were political, military, and economic leaders. Of those found guilty, a number received death sentences or life imprisonment. The second set of Nuremberg Trials dealt with lesser war criminals, including judges and doctors.

Unlike any nation before or since that has been charged with crimes against humanity, postwar Germany has engaged in a program of making reparations both to world Jewry and to the state of Israel, totaling an estimated $70 billion so far. Speaking in the Bundestag (German national parliament) on September 27, 1951, the West German chancellor Konrad Adenauer made the following declaration: "The Federal government and the great majority of the German people are deeply aware of the immeasurable suffering endured by the Jews of Germany and by the Jews of the occupied

Defendents in the Nuremberg Trials are shown circa 1945–1946, among them Hermann Göring (*front row, far left*) and Wilhelm Keitel (*front row, far right*).

territories during the period of National Socialism [Nazism] … In our name, unspeakable crimes have been committed and they demand restitution, both moral and material, for the persons and properties of the Jews who have been so seriously harmed."

In 1938, just before the outbreak of World War II, the Jewish population of the world was 16.5 million. Today, even after decades of postwar recovery, it measures 14.5 million.

After the Cambodian Genocide

Nearly twenty years were to pass after the ousting of Pol Pot's Khmer Rouge before a UN-backed war criminal court, the Extraordinary Chambers in the Courts of Cambodia (ECCC), began to try the surviving leaders of the Cambodian regime. Another ten years passed before judges were sworn in and the names of five officials were presented to them.

A major figure to be tried was the commandant of the notorious Tuol Sleng Torture Center, in which at least sixteen thousand prisoners accused of disloyalty were tortured until they were murdered or allowed to die. The prison master, who was not found and arrested until 1999, is known as Duch (pronounced "doik"), although his real name is Kaing Guek Eav.

Duch's defense, like that of lesser figures brought to trial for hideous crimes, was that he had no choice. Had he been unwilling to carry out the murders of the Tuol Sleng prisoners, he himself would have been killed. Nevertheless, he was sentenced to life in prison in 2012.

Three people have been convicted by the ECCC thus far. Several trials are still underway.

Justice for Rwanda

Justice came more swiftly for victims of the genocide in Rwanda. At the end of 1994, the year of the genocide, the UN Security Council established the International Criminal Tribunal for Rwanda (ICTR), which met in Arusha, Tanzania.

Hutu leaders finally brought to trial in 2002 included Colonel Théoneste Bagosora, who had fled to Cameroon, where he was apprehended. After five years of hearings during which Bagosora maintained his innocence, he was sentenced, in December 2008, to life in prison. The sixty-seven-year-old former army colonel was convicted of genocide, murder, extermination, rape, persecution, other inhumane acts, violence, and outrages upon personal dignity.

The court determined that Bagosora bore ultimate responsibility for the sexual assault and murder of the Hutu moderate prime minister of Rwanda, Agathe Uwilingiyimana and for the deaths of ten Belgian peacekeepers and four government opposition leaders, among his other crimes. A death sentence for Bagosora was not an option under the rules of the ICTR.

Within Rwanda, hundreds of thousands of genocide suspects have been tried in what are known as Gacaca courts. These courts have led the effort to unify and reconcile Rwanda's population by bringing those who committed genocidal acts against their neighbors to justice, largely through mandated community service. The guilty have been put to work building homes, planting crops and trees, and building roads to restore the infrastructure of the country as well as the destroyed property of the victims.

Finding a Way Forward

The world may never see an end to genocide. Racism, religious hatred, and ethnic rivalries persist in every corner of the globe. What's more, the question of the best way to address these crises when they take place still remains open for debate. Military intervention is politically difficult for the nations involved and may not always improve the situation for victims. Nonmilitary avenues help but in most cases fail to stop the violence. In the end, each conflict may have its own solution, based on its context and the actors involved. As long as all nations continue to voice a strong opposition to genocide, they may continue to seek better solutions and more effective ways to stop this egregious crime wherever it occurs.

Glossary

anti-Semitic Feeling or acting with discrimination against or hostility toward Jewish people.

barbarism An act or idea that is unacceptable or offensive to contemporary or civilized peoples.

colonialism Control or a policy advocating control by a political or national power over a region or people.

dehumanize To deprive someone of their human qualities.

dissident A person who disagrees with a dominant political or religious system.

embargo A prohibition on commerce.

en masse As a whole; in a large group.

ethnic cleansing The persecution, imprisonment, or widespread murder of an ethnic minority group.

exploit To make use of a person or thing for one's own benefit or advantage.

genocide The intentional and systematic murder of a group based on racial, ethnic, cultural, or religious prejudice.

inalienable Incapable of being surrendered or taken away.

intrinsically By its natural character.

jihad Holy war against nonbelievers of Islam.

jurisdiction The authority or power to legislate or apply the law.

multilateral Involving more than two nations or parties.

oppress To crush or silence by use of authority, influence, or power.

reparation Payment of damages.

repatriation The return of a person to his or her country of origin.

sanction An economic measure designed to force a nation to follow international law or punish it for violating international law.

smallpox A viral infection that causes pustules to appear on an infected person's skin and can be deadly.

sovereignty Supreme power over a political area or state.

subjugation The act of bringing someone or something under one's control.

triumvirate A group of three.

Further Information

Books

Bartov, Omer. *Anatomy of a Genocide: The Life and Death of a Town Called Buczacz*. New York: Simon & Schuster, 2018.

Heing, Bridey. *Ethnic Cleansing in the Syrian Civil War*. New York: Rosen Young Adult, 2018.

Suny, Ronald Grigor. *"They Can Live in the Desert but Nowhere Else": A History of the Armenian Genocide*. Princeton, NJ: Princeton University Press, 2015.

Torres, John A. *The Guatemalan Genocide of the Maya People*. New York: Rosen Young Adult, 2018.

Websites

United Nations Office on Genocide Prevention and the Responsibility to Protect

http://www.un.org/en/genocideprevention

This site offers up key foundational information on the definition of genocide according to the United Nations and shares the latest news on efforts to prevent genocide.

United States Holocaust Memorial Museum

https://www.ushmm.org

This website offers up a wealth of information and source materials on the Holocaust. It also shares information on victims and survivors and includes an encyclopedia.

Yale University Genocide Studies Program

https://gsp.yale.edu

This site features case studies; resources on prevention, trauma, and war crimes; and audiovisual resources related to genocide.

Videos

Genocide in Africa

https://www.youtube.com/watch?v=m8__o6mzsX0

This *National Geographic* video dives into the history behind and the atrocities committed during the genocide in Darfur, Sudan.

Raphael Lemkin Defines Genocide (1949)

https://www.youtube.com/watch?v=QO-Pb-T8MwM

In an interview, Raphael Lemkin explains his definition of "genocide" and why he felt that it was necessary to invent the word.

Rohingya Refugees on Myanmar's Brutal Crackdown: 'They Slaughtered Our People'

https://www.youtube.com/watch?time_continue=8&v=NxG10iTT17A

This video by the *Guardian* newspaper features interviews with refugees of the Rohingya genocide in Myanmar.

Organizations

Amnesty International

1 Easton Street
London, WC1X 0DW
United Kingdom
+44 20 74135500
http://www.amnesty.org

Amnesty International (AI) is a nongovernmental organization (NGO) that operates worldwide to end human rights violations, including genocide, torture, and the death penalty.

Canadian Centre for International Justice

312 Laurier Avenue East
Ottawa, ON K1N 1H9
Canada
(613) 230-6114
https://www.ccij.ca

This organization works to help survivors of torture and genocide find justice on the international stage.

The Enough Project

1420 K Street NW, Suite 200
Washington, DC 20005
(310) 717-0606
http://endgenocide.org

This activist organization tracks and shares information on genocides around the world. It mobilizes activism against facilitators of genocide.

European Court of Human Rights

Council of Europe
F-67075 Strasbourg cedex
France
+33 (0)3 88 41 20 18
http://echr.coe.int

European Court of Human Rights (Cour européenne des droits de l'homme, or ECtHR) has dealt with abuses by the Soviet Union and by post-Soviet Russia, by the United Kingdom in its treatment of Irish prisoners, and with other infractions committed by its European members.

Human Rights Watch

350 Fifth Avenue, 34th Floor
New York, NY 10118
(212) 290-4700
http://www.hrw.org

Human Rights Watch is a leading nongovernmental organization that promotes human rights on an international scale. It works to document and prevent genocide, torture, capital punishment, and child labor, among other causes.

United Nations High Commissioner for Refugees

Case Postale 2500
CH-1211 Genève 2 Dépôt
Switzerland
+41 22 739 8111
http://www.unhcr.org

The UNHCR protects and supports refugee victims of war, genocide, natural disasters, and other catastrophic events throughout the world. UNHCR received Nobel Peace Prizes in 1954 and 1981.

Bibliography

"About UNAMID." United Nations–African Union Hybrid Operation in Darfur, 2018. https://unamid.unmissions.org/about-unamid-0.

Adenauer, Konrad. Speech to the Bundestag, Bonn, Germany, September 27, 1951.

Agence France-Presse. "A Timeline of the Islamic State's Gains and Losses in Iraq and Syria." PRI, February 19, 2017. https://www.pri.org/stories/2017-02-19/timeline-islamic-states-gains-and-losses-iraq-and-syria.

Akçam, Taner. *A Shameful Act: The Armenian Genocide and the Question of Turkish Responsibility*. New York: Metropolitan, Henry Holt, 2006.

Ali, Rushanara. "One Year On, a Million Rohingya Refugees Still Fear for Their Lives." *Guardian*, August 16, 2018. https://www.theguardian.com/commentisfree/2018/aug/16/rohingya-refugees-bangladesh-camps-international-aid.

"Armenia Country Profile." BBC News, May 8, 2018. https://www.bbc.com/news/world-europe-17398605.

Associated Press and *Times of Israel* Staff. "Germany Agrees to $88 Million More for Holocaust Survivors." *Times of Israel*, July 10, 2018. https://www.timesofisrael.com/germany-agrees-to-88-million-more-for-holocaust-survivors.

"Aung San Suu Kyi: The Democracy Icon Who Fell from Grace." BBC News, September 13, 2018. https://www.bbc.com/news/world-asia-pacific-11685977.

Balakian, Peter. *The Burning Tigris: The Armenian Genocide and America's Response*. New York: HarperCollins, 2003.

Beaubien, Jason. "In Bangladeshi Camps, Rohingya Refugees Try to Move Forward with Their Lives." NPR, August 30, 2018. https://www.npr.org/2018/08/30/643008438/in-bangladeshi-camps-rohingya-refugees-try-to-move-forward-with-their-lives.

Beech, Hannah. "'No Such Thing as Rohingya': Myanmar Erases a History." *New York Times*, December 2, 2017. https://www.nytimes.com/2017/12/02/world/asia/myanmar-rohingya-denial-history.html.

Bellingham, Henry, MP, et al. "UN Funding Cuts Put Lives at Risk in Darfur." *Guardian*, August 1, 2017. https://www.theguardian.com/world/2017/aug/01/un-funding-cuts-put-lives-at-risk-in-darfur.

Bennet, James. "Clinton Declares U.S., with World, Failed Rwandans." *New York Times*, March 26, 1998. https://www.nytimes.com/1998/03/26/world/clinton-in-africa-the-overview-clinton-declares-us-with-world-failed-rwandans.html.

Borger, Julian, and Owen Bowcott. "Radovan Karadžlć Sentenced to 40 Years for Srebrenica Genocide." *Guardian*, March 24, 2016. https://www.theguardian.com/world/2016/mar/24/radovan-karadzic-criminally-responsible-for-genocide-at-srebenica.

Bowcott, Owen, and Julian Borger. "Ratko Mladic Convicted of War Crimes and Genocide at UN Tribunal." *Guardian*, November 22, 2017. https://www.theguardian.com/world/2017/nov/22/ratko-mladic-convicted-of-genocide-and-war-crimes-at-un-tribunal.

Burr, J. Millard, and Robert O. Collins. *Darfur: The Long Road to Disaster*. Princeton, NJ: Markus Wiener, 2006.

Callimachi, Rukmini. "Freed from ISIS, Yazidi Women Return in 'Severe Shock.'" *New York Times*, July 27, 2017. https://www.nytimes.com/2017/07/27/world/middleeast/isis-yazidi-women-rape-iraq-mosul-slavery.html.

"Cambodia 1975–1979." United States Holocaust Memorial Museum. Accessed October 19, 2018. https://www.ushmm.org/confront-genocide/cases/cambodia/introduction/cambodia-1975.

"Cambodian Genocide." World Without Genocide, Mitchell Hamline School of Law, May 2018. http://worldwithoutgenocide.org/genocides-and-conflicts/cambodia.

Canal, Gabriella. "Rohingya Muslims Are the Most Persecuted Minority in the World: Who Are They?" Global Citizen, February 10, 2017. https://www.globalcitizen.org/en/content/recognizing-the-rohingya-and-their-horrifying-pers.

Carroll, Rory. "US Chose to Ignore Rwandan Genocide." *Guardian*, March 31, 2004. https://www.theguardian.com/world/2004/mar/31/usa.rwanda.

"Clinic Study Finds Evidence of Genocide in Myanmar." Yale Law School, October 29, 2015. https://law.yale.edu/yls-today/news/clinic-study-finds-evidence-genocide-myanmar.

Cooper, Helene, Mark Landler, and Alissa J. Rubin. "Obama Allows Limited Airstrikes on ISIS." *New York Times*, August 7, 2014. https://www.nytimes.com/2014/08/08/world/middleeast/obama-weighs-military-strikes-to-aid-trapped-iraqis-officials-say.html.

Dearden, Lizzie. "Almost 10,000 Yazidis 'Killed or Kidnapped in Isis Genocide but True Scale of Horror May Never Be Known.'" *Independent* (UK), May 9, 2017. https://www.independent.co.uk/news/world/middle-east/isis-islamic-state-yazidi-sex-slaves-genocide-sinjar-death-toll-number-kidnapped-study-un-lse-a7726991.html.

Dewan, Angela. "Who Are the Rohingya and Why Are They Fleeing?" CNN, September 13, 2017. https://www.cnn.com/2017/09/05/asia/rohingya-myanmar-explainer/index.html.

Fanon, Frantz. *The Wretched of the Earth*. New York: Grove Press, 2004.

"General Guilty of Bosnia Genocide." BBC News, August 2, 2001. http://news.bbc.co.uk/2/hi/europe/ 1470928.stm.

"Genocide in Guatemala (1981–1983)." Holocaust Museum Houston. Accessed October 18, 2018. https://www.hmh.org/la_Genocide_Guatemala.shtml.

Gilbert, Martin. *Auschwitz and the Allies*. New York: Holt, Rinehart and Winston, 1981.

Gourevitch, Philip. *We Wish to Inform You That Tomorrow We Will Be Killed with Our Families: Stories from Rwanda*. New York: Farrar, Straus, 1998.

Griffiths, James. "UN Calls for Genocide Tribunal over Rohingya Crisis." CNN, September 18, 2018. https://edition.cnn.com/2018/09/18/asia/myanmar-united-nations-report-intl/index.html.

Harris, Chris. "Three Survivors of the Srebrenica Massacres Tell Their Stories." EuroNews, October 7, 2015. https://www.euronews.com/2015/07/10/personal-stories-from-three-survivors-of-the-srebrenica-massacres.

"Head of Human Rights Fact-Finding Mission on Myanmar Urges Security Council to Ensure Accountability for Serious Violations Against Rohingya." United Nations, October 24, 2018. https://www.un.org/press/en/2018/sc13552.doc.htm.

History.com editors. "Bosnian Genocide." History.com, August 21, 2018. https://www.history.com/topics/1990s/bosnian-genocide.

Holbrooke, Richard. *To End a War*. New York: Random House, 1998.

Jalabi, Raya. "Who Are the Yazidis and Why Is Isis Hunting Them?" *Guardian*, August 11, 2014. https://www.theguardian.com/world/2014/aug/07/who-yazidi-isis-iraq-religion-ethnicity-mountains.

Jett, Jennifer. "Canada Revokes Honorary Citizenship of Aung San Suu Kyi." *New York Times*, October 3, 2018. https://www. nytimes.com/2018/10/03/world/asia/aung-san-suu-kyi-canada-citizenship.html.

Kazi Fahmida, Farzana. "The 'Floating People' of Myanmar: How Rohingya Refugees Reclaim Their Identity Through Art and Song." Conversation, February 9, 2017. http://theconversation. com/the-floating-people-of-myanmar-how-rohingya-refugees-reclaim-their-identity-through-art-and-song-72341.

Koppisch, John. "Why Are Indian Reservations So Poor? A Look at the Bottom 1%." *Forbes*, December 13, 2011. https://www. forbes.com/sites/johnkoppisch/2011/12/13/why-are-indian-reservations-so-poor-a-look-at-the-bottom-1/#79b1bbe93c07.

Landler, Mark. "Myanmar's Crackdown on Rohingya Is Ethnic Cleansing, Tillerson Says." *New York Times*, November 22, 2017. https://www.nytimes.com/2017/11/22/us/politics/tillerson-myanmar-rohingya-ethnic-cleansing. html?module=inline.

Laughland, Oliver, and Tom Silverstone. "Liquid Genocide: Alcohol Destroyed Pine Ridge Reservation—Then They Fought Back." *Guardian*, September 29, 2017. https://www.theguardian. com/society/2017/sep/29/pine-ridge-indian-reservation-south-dakota.

Lewy, Guenter. "Were American Indians the Victims of Genocide?" History News Network, September 2004. https:// historynewsnetwork.org/article/7302.

Lone, Wa, and Shoon Naing. "At Least 71 Killed in Myanmar as Rohingya Insurgents Stage Major Attack." Reuters, August 24, 2017. https://www.reuters.com/article/us-myanmar-rohingya/at-least-71-killed-in-myanmar-as-rohingya-insurgents-stage-major-attack-idUSKCN1B507K.

Lowe, Rebecca. "'Deals with the Devil Always Unravel': The UK Blind Spot for Sudan's Abuses." *Guardian*, April 24, 2018. https://www.theguardian.com/global-development/2018/apr/24/uk-blind-spot-sudan-human-rights-abuses.

Luft, Aliza. "What We, as Citizens, Can Do to Fight Genocide." *Washington Post*, January 26, 2018. https://www.washingtonpost.com/news/democracy-post/wp/2018/01/26/what-we-as-citizens-can-do-to-fight-genocide/?utm_term=.cb3d18238deb.

Morgenthau, Henry Sr. *Ambassador Morgenthau's Story*. New York: Doubleday and Doran, 1918.

Moses, A. Dirk, ed. *Genocide and Settler Society: Frontier Violence and Stolen Indigenous Children in Australian History*. New York: Berghahn Books, 2004.

"Myanmar Rohingya Militants Arsa Vow to Fight on After Attack." BBC News, January 7, 2018. https://www.bbc.com/news/world-asia-42595275.

"Myanmar Rohingya: What You Need to Know About the Crisis." BBC News, April 24, 2018. https://www.bbc.com/news/world-asia-41566561.

"Myanmar: What Sparked Latest Violence in Rakhine?" BBC News, September 19, 2017. https://www.bbc.com/news/world-asia-41082689.

Mydans, Seth. "Ex-Khmer Rouge Leader Blames U.S." *New York Times*, November 23, 2011. https://www.nytimes.com/2011/11/24/world/asia/ex-khmer-rouge-leader-blames-us.html.

NPR, Robert Wood Johnson Foundation, and Harvard T. H. Chan School of Public Health. "Discrimination in America: Experiences and Views of Native Americans." NPR, November 2017. https://www.npr.org/documents/2017/nov/NPR-discrimination-native-americans-final.pdf.

Ostler, Jeffrey. "Genocide and American Indian History." *Oxford Research Encyclopedias: American History*. March 2015. http://americanhistory.oxfordre.com/view/10.1093/acrefore/9780199329175.001.0001/acrefore-9780199329175-e-3.

"Powell Declares Killing in Darfur 'Genocide.'" *Online NewsHour*, PBS.org, September 9, 2004. http://www.pbs.org/newshour/updates/sudan_09-09-04.html.

Power, Samantha. *"A Problem from Hell": America and the Age of Genocide*. New York: HarperCollins Perennial, 2003.

———. "Bystanders to Genocide." *Atlantic*, September 2001. https://www.theatlantic.com/magazine/archive/2001/09/bystanders-to-genocide/304571.

Prunier, Gérard. *Darfur: The Ambiguous Genocide*. Ithaca, NY: Cornell University Press, revised and updated edition, 2007.

———. *The Rwanda Crisis: History of a Genocide*. New York: Columbia University Press, 1995.

"Ratko Mladic Jailed for Life over Bosnia War Genocide." BBC News, November 22, 2017. https://www.bbc.com/news/world-europe-42080090.

Rieff, David. *Slaughterhouse: Bosnia and the Failure of the West*. New York: Simon & Schuster, 1995.

Saccaro, Matt. "This Is What Modern Day Discrimination Against Native Americans Looks Like." Mic, October 20, 2014. https://mic.com/articles/101804/this-is-what-modern-day-discrimination-against-native-americans-looks-like#.8eBPteOjb.

Salopek, Paul. "A Century Later, Slaughter Still Haunts Turkey and Armenia." *National Geographic*, April 2016. https://www.nationalgeographic.com/magazine/2016/04/armenia-massacre-turkey-kurds-history/?user.testname=none.

Semega, Jessica L., Kayla R. Fontenot, and Melissa A. Kollar. "Income and Poverty in the United States: 2016." United States Census Bureau, September 12, 2017. https://www.census.gov/library/publications/2017/demo/p60-259.html.

Seybolt, Taylor B. "Humanitarian Intervention and International Security." *Oxford Research Encyclopedia of International Studies*, March 2010. http://internationalstudies.oxfordre.com/view/10.1093/acrefore/9780190846626.001.0001/acrefore-

9780190846626-e-217#acrefore-9780190846626-e-217-div1-0004.

Short, Philip. *Pol Pot: Anatomy of a Nightmare*. New York: Henry Holt, 2004.

Silber, Laura, and Allan Little. *Yugoslavia: Death of a Nation*. New York: Penguin, 1996.

Stannard, David E. *American Holocaust: The Conquest of the New World*. New York: Oxford University Press, 1992.

Steidle, Brian, and Gretchen Steidle Wallace. *The Devil Came on Horseback: Bearing Witness to the Genocide in Darfur*. New York: Public Affairs, Perseus, 2007.

"The Story Of ... Smallpox — and Other Deadly Eurasian Germs." PBS, 2005. https://www.pbs.org/gunsgermssteel/variables/smallpox.html.

"Sudan-Darfur (2003 — First Combat Deaths)." Project Ploughshares, January 23, 2018. http://ploughshares.ca/pl_armedconflict/sudan-darfur-2003-first-combat-deaths.

Taylor, Adam. "Why the World Should Not Forget Khmer Rouge and the Killing Fields of Cambodia." *Washington Post*, August 7, 2014. https://www.washingtonpost.com/news/worldviews/wp/2014/08/07/why-the-world-should-not-forget-khmer-rouge-and-the-killing-fields-of-cambodia/?noredirect=on&utm_term=.c19929096ba6.

Taylor, Alan. *American Colonies: The Settling of North America*. New York: Penguin Books, 2001.

"10 Days in Iraq: Aid Drops, Air-Strikes and 200,000 New Refugees." BBC News, August 19, 2014. https://www.bbc.com/news/world-middle-east-28761383.

Than, Ker. "Massive Population Drop Found for Native Americans, DNA Shows." *National Geographic*, December 5, 2011. https://news.nationalgeographic.com/news/2011/12/111205-native-americans-europeans-population-dna-genetics-science.

Tran, Mark. "Victims of Darfur Atrocities Find a Voice." *Guardian*, July 22, 2008. https://www.theguardian.com/world/2008/jul/22/sudan.

"United States Citizenship for the Native American." Library of Congress. Accessed October 18, 2018. http://www.loc.gov/teachers/classroommaterials/presentationsandactivities/presentations/immigration/native_american8.html.

UN Office for the Coordination of Humanitarian Affairs. "Sudan: Darfur Humanitarian Overview (1 February 2018)." ReliefWeb, February 28, 2018. https://reliefweb.int/report/sudan/sudan-darfur-humanitarian-overview-1-february-2018.

"Vital Statistics: Jewish Population of the World." Jewish Virtual Library, 2017. https://www.jewishvirtuallibrary.org/jewish-population-of-the-world.

"Warrant Issued for Sudan's Leader." BBC News, March 4, 2009. http://news.bbc.co.uk/2/hi/africa/7923102.stm.

Westcott, Ben, and Rebecca Wright. "Suu Kyi: Myanmar Needs 'National Reconciliation and Peace.'" CNN, November 30, 2016. https://www.cnn.com/2016/11/30/asia/aung-san-suu-kyi-kofi-annan-myanmar/index.html.

"What Guilt Does the U.S. Bear in Guatemala?" *New York Times*, May 19, 2013. https://www.nytimes.com/roomfordebate/2013/05/19/what-guilt-does-the-us-bear-in-guatemala.

"Who Are the Rohingya?" Al Jazeera, April 18, 2018. https://www.aljazeera.com/indepth/features/2017/08/rohingya-muslims-170831065142812.html.

Wintour, Patrick. "Myanmar Rohingya Crisis: ICC Begins Inquiry into Atrocities." *Guardian*, September 19, 2018. https://www.theguardian.com/world/2018/sep/19/myanmar-rohingya-crisis-icc-begins-investigation-into-atrocities.

Wright, Rebecca, and Joshua Berlinger. "Hundreds of Armed Men Attack Police in Myanmar; UN Calls for Restraint." CNN, October 12, 2016. https://www.cnn.com/2016/10/12/asia/myanmar-violence.

Zygielbojm, Szmul. "Pole's Suicide Note Pleads for Jews." *New York Times*, June 4, 1943.

Index

Page numbers in **boldface** refer to images.

About the Authors

Lila Perl published more than sixty books for young people and adults, including fiction and nonfiction. Her nonfiction writings were mainly in the fields of social history, family memoir, and biography. Two of her books were honored with American Library Association Notable awards. Ten titles were selected as Notable Children's Trade Books in the Field of Social Studies. Lila Perl also received a Boston Globe Horn Book Award, a Sidney Taylor Committee Award, and a Young Adults' Choice Award from the International Reading Association. The New York Public Library has cited her work among Best Books for the Teen Age.

Erin L. McCoy is a literature, language, and cultural studies educator and an award-winning photojournalist and poet. She holds a master of arts degree in Hispanic studies and a master of fine arts degree in creative writing from the University of Washington. She has edited more than two dozen nonfiction books for young adults, including *The Mexican-American War*, *The Israel-Palestine Border Conflict*, and *Poverty: Public Crisis or Private Struggle?* from Cavendish Square Publishing. She is from Louisville, Kentucky.